Extolling the Ordinary

Kevin Thompson

Editor Matthew DeCapua

Extolling the Ordinary
Copyright JUNE 2021
By Kevin E. Thompson
Editor: Matthew DeCapua
Cover Art & Design by the Author

Inspiration

When life held troubled times, and had me down on my knees
There's always been someone. to come along and comfort me
A kind word from a stranger, to lend a helping hand
A phone call from a friend, just to say, I understand
But ain't it kind of funny, at the dark end of the road
That someone lights the way, with just a single ray of hope
Oh I believe there are angels among us
Sent down to us from somewhere up above
They come to you and me, in our darkest hours
To show us how to live, to teach us how to give
To guide us with the light of love

ANGELS AMONG US
by Becky Hobbs and
Don Goodman

...and so the title and theme of my first book, *Etchings on Angel Wings* came to light. The lyrics and ideology of this song most sums up my basic life philosophy. I believe highly in the goodness of mankind and treasure the stories, songs and views that preserve the sometimes frail acceptance of life in that most simplistic understanding. *Extolling the Ordinary* carries on what was started.

Dedication

Here comes Panda
Coming to Amanda
Take his little hand
And we'll go sit
On the veranda
There we'll sit
In blissful
Hand in hand
And it's me
And Amanda
And her Panda
Just me
and Amanda and her Panda

MANDY'S SONG
Words and Music by
Kevin E Thompson
written in the fall of 1988

This one is for Mandy
Because she is so much more than ordinary and
makes everything in my life worthwhile.

Table of Contents

Inspiration
Page iii

Dedication
Page v

Foreword
Page xi

Introduction
Page 1

Cat Tales
Page 11

Astronaut Dreams
Page 13

Atticus' Story
Page 17

Guarding the Crown Jewels
Page 31

EXTOLLING THE ORDINARY

Fantasy
Page 43

Admitted Fantasies
Page 45

The Spirit of Inanimate Things
Page 59

A Dichotomy of Longings
Page 75

Dreams
Page 79

My All-time Favorite Dream
Page 81

Return Visit From A Beloved Friend
Page 85

Lost in "The Emotional Mall of America"
Page 89

Feelings
Page 95

March 15, 2021
Page 97

Kevin Thompson

On The Other Side of Alone
Page 99

Why I Cry
Page 109

Going Out to Sea
Page 113

The Big "D": an essay
Page 117

Withering
Page 129

Truth
Page 135

Before I Trusted Karma
Page 137

Novembers
Page 151

The Good-bye
Page 153

Seasonal Surrender
Page 159

EXTOLLING THE ORDINARY

Chadwick Boseman & Judy Holliday
Page 161

Where I Live
Page 175

"Broad Stripes and Bright Stars"
Page 185

The Mighty Oak
Page 193

Angels, Shrinks & Revelations
Page 211

Fiction
Page 239

Forever
Page 241

Afterword
Page 257

About the Author
Page 263

Foreword

We could all use a lighthouse about now.

It's been a long pandemic. We've oscillated between certainty and doubt, science and fiction, boredom and panic. We have stared into the void of the Netflix menu until it stared back. We realize now that we spent most of our lives ignorant of the true meaning of the phrase, "cabin fever."

We're cautiously emerging from under the rocks we've been hiding, optimistic (and maybe a little desperate), blinking back the glorious sunlight, wary of Delta variants, but all too eager to get out there, to re-engage with the world. It's a raw and vulnerable moment. To repeat, we could all use a lighthouse about now.

Enter *Extolling the Ordinary*.

As we weigh anchor and get underway, we each run the very real risk of stimulus overload. We have family and friends with whom, at long last, to reunite, we have trips to take, theater to see, restaurants to enjoy (remember those?), museums to visit, subways to ride, crowds to move in, lines to get into, eighteen months of inertia to make up for. *We have places to go and things to do!* Like, right now! Let's go!

And, yet.

And, yet, gentle reader, and yet - we must not lose ourselves in this rush to movement, or forget the hard-won lessons of this not-quite-over pandemic, or fool ourselves into believing that The Before Times can be restored just as we remember them.

Though we may ache to run - and we shall! - we must also find the time to feel our feet on the ground even as we delight at the wind in our maskless faces.

Here, in his second book, Kevin has found an even deeper profundity to his mesmerizing literary voice and, in so doing, shared with us a priceless gift at a vital moment - an enduring and beatific appreciation for that which is too often, and at our own great peril, taken for granted.

By all means, throw the throttle wide open, point your nose into the wind, and sail fast and free! But as you do, look landward from time to time and check your bearing against these luminous lighthouse pages of Kevin's unequaled powers of story. Adventure calls, but watch that you don't lose yourself. Kevin will see to it, if you'll let him.

You've got your lighthouse.

Boldly go,

Matthew DeCapua
Editor

Introduction

> *Not all dreams are great big dreams*
> *Some people's dreams are small*
> *Not all dreams have to have a golden fleece*
> *Or any kind of fleece at all*
> *My dreams like my name are very plain*
> *No shining knight must kneel*
> *My dreams like my name are very plain*
> *But nevertheless they're real*
> *They're all so very real*
> *...*
> *Simple little dreams will do.*
>
> SIMPLE LITTLE THINGS
> From *110 In The Shade*
> By Tom Jones and Harvey Schmidt

I hadn't planned on becoming a writer. Well, at least not at the time I put my toes in the water and suddenly ended up swimming. There was a plan to write a play that has been in my head for the past twenty years. But that was a plan for my retirement from working as a talent rep. And yes, there has been on-going chatter ever since I can remember of chronicling a collection of humorous happenings shared with my former wife. The pressure for that seems to have increased among friends and my daughter's friends who clamor to hear the retelling of those accounts like small children beg to hear their favorite fairy tale over and over and over again. I suppose I will get to that task in the near future before the verbal retelling distorts the simple events into comic operas of disproportionate contemporary folklore. Like in all tales, ardent truth is what makes them worth the telling.

And there I go again. I'm meandering from the place I was heading to. That happens to me when my hand picks up a pencil and begins thinking out-loud on a legal pad or my clumsy arthritic fingers find their way onto the keyboard of my computer. There are so many directions in which I can go and much to my frustration and delight, I want to go in all of them - sadly, sometimes all at once. Often I end up in a different place than where I aimed my journey. And I have learned to live with myself over this enigmatic predicament I so often find myself embroiled within. It seems to be the unique and personally peculiar paradox of my writing technique. I have learned to find my way back to the major highways of my literary travel explorations without a compass. I never feel like I am lost, or even getting lost for that matter. Just as I believe that the energy of angels guide us through our life, I also believe and have come to learn, even when behind the wheel of an automobile, all roads eventually connect. You will find your way home. And sometimes even though it takes more time than you planned for, you will get where you headed out to be.

And for me, what I learn along the way is invaluable. By veering off the route my map has told me to follow, I am awakened to hidden thoughts and ideas I thought I misplaced or maybe put in some *wrong file* or left in that pile of clutter I let pile up in some unused corner of my brain. Often the surprise findings will feed the intent of my story in ways I hadn't arranged or planned. Sometimes they simply become the catalyst for a whole new idea. Many times they become the better foundation for the rewrite of what I had set out to uncover in my story.

Etchings On Angel Wings was originally planned as a series of anecdotal pieces about dealing with challenges of entering the time of the Covid-19 pandemic. When I started out writing the anthology I had no idea at that time, the world would be living in the confines of the crisis for so long a period of time and would extend and go on as long as it has. The reality of what was happening around everyone changed the perceptions each person had in coping-with and managing their way of dealing with their situations. Over time everyone adjusted and readjusted, accepted and dismissed, agreed and disagreed with what they were facing. The passing of time and the introduction of new elements and discoveries reshaped things as they progressed.

My book was intended to be humorous. But actually living through the events, my ability to find enough humor in what was going on diminished significantly and I found myself far off the path of where I intended to take my casual literary stroll. I wasn't lost but I discovered things about my wanting to be a writer and putting forth ideas that I felt were valuable enough to share. The "Covid Tales" in *Etchings On Angel Wings,* as they ended up being called, turned out to be only a small part of what I was wanting to voice. *Nineteen Covid Tales* was a completed journey before it achieved its intention. And my going off the path allowed me to test *my* "wings" as a newly-declared writer.

Once I gave myself license to widen my horizon for the book it became a better journey; at least, one more comfortable and fun for me. The opportunity gave me the freedom to explore topics and ideas that I was yearning to express in this newly adopted form of creative expression. There is a file of incomplete and right-out-dud stories and poems on my computer. But I amazed myself in finding that the topics that were easiest to articulate and the ones that I was able to give a shape and life to, were not about what I thought would be my arena for topics - theater and the entertainment business, the very place I have dwelt throughout my entire adult life.

My stories and poems that most validated me ended up being about things that grew from my feelings about life itself. Things I learned from people, or just having special people in my life, held more substance and truth than the accounts of events that provided my sustenance and livelihood for close to fifty years. And as I opened myself up more and more to the things that were essential to who I am, I found my voice as a writer - well, at least I was learning to speak, even if the voice still cracked here and there, exposing the truth of my immaturity as a writer.

Wandering from the path is a key part of who I am. I like learning and experiencing new things. I don't like watching a movie for a second time. I absolutely detest having to sit through a re-run of a television episode. I rarely will re-read a book. Being a man of the theater, I do revisit plays and productions. Part of my enchantment with theater is the fragility of the moment by moment explosion of words, performance and visuals amidst the many reactions of living bodies around one as each intakes moments that can never be repeated again. There is something divinely precious in that. Even if a play or production is not particularly good - or downright bad for that matter - I experience total sensory catharsis that always leaves deep emotional tattoos on my soul. And every moment is a wandering of going off the path into something new.

Writing my first book was a close facsimile to that experience. And the feedback from readers was the most rewarding element. I know some people were too kind out of politeness. And there were people who articulated little but expressed an overall enjoyment or appreciation for what they read. Those who have still remained silent continually command the most of my respect because there is something wonderful in not really knowing what people genuinely think. A few people rendered some harsh criticism but did so in a respectful manner which also won my keen attention. So many people encouraged me to write a second book. I am hoping it is because they enjoyed the experience of the first book and are eager to see what new ideas might come. And undoubtedly there are those among that crowd who said that in hopes that the second attempt might be better or more worthy of their engagement.

I always planned for there to be another book. The self-satisfaction I got from writing the first emboldened me to give myself permission to do it all again regardless of public or private opinion. I thank those who actually encouraged me to write this second volume regardless of the intent behind it.

Brace yourselves, dear readers because you are about to endure another escapade of how I go off the tracks and end up on another path.

I had chosen a title for book number two. *Nascent* was the title. I know, I know…Why? Why pick an uncommon word that most people may not know or if they do, may not know its precise meaning? I chose it because it best expresses the way I feel about myself as a writer - particularly of this second book. And because

I am proud of all the honesty in my writing, I confess that the somewhat pretentiousness of a somewhat obscure word appealed to me. Karma will one day get me for such hidden vanities. But the word is an adjective. It means - being born, in its most simplistic use - a rebirth in a deeper sense.

I felt this most exemplified both my place and the nature of my writing as I entered a more confident air about defining myself as a writer. It was a simple one word statement. It was a word of a certain complexity and probably it was most likely suitable because the word itself was off the beaten path - that place I keep telling you I like to wander off to. The new stories and poems come from new inspirations and reveal, hopefully, a deeper sharing of myself with readers. *Nascent.* It was locked in. And then things started happening as I ventured into sharing the gifts I wanted to surrender to my readers.

I wouldn't say I lost confidence in myself but I did start to question what made the things I write about worth sharing and reading. What is it in the very voice of what I project that demanded my recognition?

A number of folks told me what they liked about my writing but mostly they talked about a particular story or a clever phrase. I started viewing the sales pages of various books on Amazon, my publishing company. I decided to reread my own promotional blurb and my

EXTOLLING THE ORDINARY

eyes wandered down the page to the section of public reviews from readers.

My longtime friend and mentor, Patricia Ryan Madson, an internationally recognized author herself, had written something in her review of *Etchings,* that I was very touched by when I read it. It validated me. It was a clear sense of being understood in what I had set out to accomplish as a new writer. A friend had said he was confused by the statement, because when he read the endorsement of the book, he was confused how she could say how much she liked the book but then negate the praise with what to him was an undercutting statement. To him "ordinary"meant it was somehow "not special enough." To me "ordinary" is that which describes things that are most precious and frail to me.

My dear friend had understood the heart of my tales and poems when she wrote:

"What I love about this book is it's ordinariness."

And there it was - clearly stated - about the things I embrace as a writer.

There are no forced or calculated mechanics constructing the stories, poems and essays I compose. They are simply told in an honest everyday kind of way. This *is* what I do. I'm not so sure I fully understood this on my own but it rang true and I was happy to own it and claim it as my place as a writer.

Relaxing into this, I began to understand what my second book was to be about, and things leaned into a new direction. Surprise? No not really. I am well-acquainted with my inclinations toward discovering something new and unique about something I was fairly sure I had a complete grasp on.

While the book remains the path of being born anew into the world of writing, I decided to share it's aim to my readers by granting the volume a new title that would let new readers and readers of my first book know what was happening between the front and back covers. And so I christened it with a new title explaining what I do,

Extolling the Ordinary

Like the first book the contents are still of the kind that I declared etched in time on the wings of angels. And music still remains the lasting angelic voice in inspiring me. As I find my way through my daily life, I am hopeful these new tales of *Etchings on Angel Wings* will hold their place with all of the others and all the stories of everyone's lives that are cherished and protected by the angels who wander about us in this world.

Sadly, there is one entry in my new book that will not be etched on any angel wings.

EXTOLLING THE ORDINARY

To be inscribed there, a story must be true and from the history of a living being.

While I am proud of the last entry in my new book, it actually does not qualify for the librarianship of my beloved winged guardians. It is a work of fiction. There are no connections to my life or of any living person's history. It is my first short story of the fictional nature. No doubt the story has all the elements of belief and human understanding I take great pride in holding as my ethical center. It is very real to me because it is a first child of sorts and I am happy to share it with you all.

I hope you smile and laugh and shed tears of joy as you experience the *ordinary* as I attempt to share it with you.

Cat Tales

Astronaut Dreams

> *And I think it's gonna be a long long time*
> *'Till touchdown brings me 'round again to find*
> *I'm not the man they think I am at home*
> *Oh no, no no*
> *I'm a rocket man*
> *Rocket man burning out his fuse up here alone*
>
> ROCKET MAN (I Think It's Gonna
Be A Long, Long Time)
by Elton John

Eyes focused upward
Always to the sky
Or beyond the ceiling

Anything above that sparkles
Catches or gives off light
Spinning wild dreams
Of life above gravity

He sits by the window
By day he envies birds
At night it is the moon

EXTOLLING THE ORDINARY

Particles of dust
Float in beams of light
Sunlight or lamplight
Becoming galaxies of stars

His need to rise
To conquer distance
With space his only challenge
He dreams of a life unknown

At times he flies
He gains that thrust
To propel upward
To seize that far-off place

The thrill of elevation
To see it all
From above
Is his only thought

You can see it in his eyes
In his position
In his ever reaching stretch
To claim that distant place

I know he sees
Far further than I
Stars and worlds
Still yet unknown

Kevin Thompson

His launches often fail
But still determination grows
He knows
Failure is not an option

He *will* get there
…that top shelf
…that very upper ledge
That hugs the ceiling

I know once it is achieved
It will not just end there
His feline dreams
To be an astronaut.

Atticus' Story

You don't own me
I'm not just one of your many toys...
So just let me be myself
That's all I ask of you
I'm young and I love to be young
I'm free and I love to be free
To say and do whatever I please

YOU DON'T OWN ME
by John L. Medora and David White

Hello. My name is Atticus. You probably hear that, and then think, "Well someone was pretty hoity-toity to lay that name on you!" It wouldn't have been my choice but considering some of the stupid names people give to their cats and other pets, I'm a whole helluva lot less embarrassed touting that choice than what I suppose I could have been saddled with.

I am what human's call a "rescu*ed* cat." I imagine you all think that I should be somehow grateful that someone took me in to offer me food and shelter and a few playthings. But let's get real. I'm a cat! That sort of sentimental hogwash just is not in the DNA of us feline creatures. OK. Maybe I am just a teeny-weeny, itsy-bitsy relieved that fate fell to me in this way. But I am not going to go all out and throw a party over the event.

The human story is that I was found under a bridge in New Jersey. Alone. And I guess if I am to be honest about it - all that is true. I was taken to an animal shelter to be given a shot at my nine lives. To my luck there was a mama cat there who just had a litter and she was impervious to me joining her litter in the suckling thing for me to get nourishment. *That* is something I am actually grateful for.

I was older than her actual offspring so it was somewhat obvious that I would be the first of that suckling gang to be whisked off to some strange home. Or, if fate wanted to be unkind, I could have been scheduled for an unwanted vacation to China, Japan, Korea or another country in the Far East. You see that's what humans feel is their right to do when an animal is deemed unwanted. They send them away to some kind of horrible camp that they call a place for, "youth in Asia." Well that would be the English choice of words. It is said that when that becomes your fate you are never heard from again following one horrendous cat scream in the night. So I guess I am glad I didn't have to take the flight to the mysterious East.

The person who claimed me was a female human. She was kind. She took me to her home in Connecticut (which to many is another hoity-toity place where you can end up with a far more embarrassing name, like Chatsworth. Or if they really want to separate your status from their human superiority, they might be cute and just call you, Catsworth.) But this young woman didn't live in the financially elevated lair part of that place. She lived in a quiet suburban blue collar setting with her Mom, her boyfriend, two other feline folks and a very hyper canine.

They were all very nice but I was sequestered from the other felines and the canine. I was kept in a separate room so the other beasts could not get to me and I could not get to them. When I was granted the freedom to explore and see the outer quarters of the house, the other animals were locked in other rooms. The nice lady was overprotective of me. I suspect she was equally as overprotective of the other non humans she kept.

At night, the boyfriend would sleep on the floor of my lockup room so that I wouldn't be alone. He let me sleep on his carrying thing I heard humans call a backpack. And he would let me crawl on him and bite and scratch him. I mean I was only a few weeks old and following my basic instincts of being a cat. I didn't know it wasn't ok to scratch and bite humans. When I was with the suckling gang, that's the sort of thing we all did all the time with each other. It's how we play! But this human was ok - he let me be myself. In retrospect I figure it was because he too was a male and he just got it.

EXTOLLING THE ORDINARY

After a few days, I was put back into the gray screened carrying bag that I had been put in to bring me to Connecticut. I wasn't sure what this meant but all the humans were pretty decent so I didn't sense any need to panic - only the continuing urge to exercise my high level of frisky activity which was stifled by being forced into what for all intents and purposes is a designer prison bag.

The young woman would talk to me and told me we were going to a place called New York. I guess we drove through it on the way from New Jersey to Connecticut. If this place was so nice, why didn't we stop and visit there on our previous journey? I have to admit there was something in all of this that was giving me pause. And *my* paws were itching to be ready for whatever was coming my way.

There was talk of something called Father's Day and how I was the big surprise for the young woman's father. I didn't know what a father was. Still don't really know. I mean I never knew my father - I guess I had one. And reviewing the facts of my short life, I really didn't know my mother either. I guess I had one but it's all a blur as to what led to my being on my own under that bridge in New Jersey. And even the whole idea of a mother-thing - am I supposed to have some sense of what it is? I certainly know what it is not! Abandoned under a bridge - found by a person who abandoned me by taking me to a shelter - where the people there pawned me off on an exhausted mama cat who just had five kittens who were gnawing away constantly on her nipples and had another one thrown into the mix - I have no notion of what this mothering thing is all about. And then, after they took me to this place to have my balls cut off, they ship me off with a strange but nice lady from Connecticut. And people wonder why cats are often crazy!

And now I was being taken to whatever a father is to be given to him and to live there in another new state called New York. During my stay in Connecticut I was taken to a place where these other womenfolk, called veterinarians, stuck me with needles. Maybe going to live with a father, which I was guessing was a male, would be a turn for the better. After all, the one human who let me be myself was the guy who slept on a floor with me so that I wouldn't be alone.

Deep breath - and a cat yawn.

Now there was something ominous about this whole gifting thing that was happening that I couldn't quite sink a cat claw or a kitten tooth into. But as the humans unpacked, a kitty-condo, bags of food, a hefty box of kitty-litter, a three piece litter box and my tiny little self in the grey prison bag, from the car, a mounting anxiety was permeating the scene. I am a cat. Anxiety is a major component of our energy. We cats can hide it well - humans…not so much. While I couldn't define or really know for certain what all the tension was about, I began to surmise that there was concern that the father-guy might not be open to having a lovable little fur-ball like myself imposed upon his life.

Panic. Maybe this was the waiting line for my ticket on that oneway flight on Korean Airlines.

The nice Connecticut lady approached the apartment door and when it opened she said, "Happy Father's Day! This is the big surprise I have been telling you about." There was a bit of a silence in the air as my temporary rescuer and her Mother looked intensely for a response from the guy at the door.

No one knows for sure what his reaction was. It was a profound stillness. It was a wrinkle in time. It was a seismic shift in this man's psyche and understanding of the world. But here I was being taken out of the bag - and now that the surprise - the cat - was out of the bag, he took me from her in his hands and started to pet my back as I held my ground and gently bit and scratched him.

It was a test. And when I graded it, I would say I gave him a C+. He was kind and I could tell he was open to having his life altered by my joining it. So maybe a B- would be a fairer grade.

"What do you want to name him?" His daughter asked him. "I'm not sure," he responded. But the daughter was insisting he make a decision. The shelter had called me Cookie and that's what the Connecticut crowd had been calling me. Not much better than Catsworth in my opinion and actually a little effeminate for a rough and tumble boy cat like me. I was eager to have that taken off the table as an idea. "Well, I had recently thought lately, if I were to get a dog, I would like to call him, Levi. It's a strong name and it has meanings of kindness," the father-guy said. "Oh, boy!" I thought to myself - "what kind of weirdo is this guy?"

Then he said, " I don't think this little guy is rugged enough for that name. He is a boy though, isn't he?" "Yes, he is a male," he was told. "How insulting! Not rugged enough! OK, I know they cut off my male appendage and when you look at me, you really can't tell for sure but Cats Almighty! Do you have to be cruel about it?!"

Then he said, "Well I think Atticus will fit him." "Your favorite literary character," his daughter said. "Yup," he said " a noble forthright soul." And the daughter said, "I thought you would call him that. I would have named him for you with that name if the choice were mine."

And so I accepted the name as it also seemed like an apology for the previous indignity thrown my way regarding Levi.

Where he lived was far tinier than the home I had just come from and the small space was filled with many things for me to explore. He let me roam freely, only stopping me when it looked like I might disappear into a place where no one could reach me easily.

The tension of the humans dwindled and while the nice lady from Connecticut seemed to have a challenging time relinquishing me to his care she eventually left and here I was - alone again - but not really - but nonetheless facing a new environment with yet another human that I would need to decipher.

When we were left alone he was gentle and wanted to hold me. But face it, I'm a cat. I make those decisions and it is important right off the bat that this guy learns the score. Cats only want to be held when they want to be held. This I would ensure he got into his nerdy, pseudo-academic head.

I knew I had my challenges cut out for me. This after all, was a *dog* person. And I knew because of that he would treat me like a dog. He'd want me to come when he called me and do tricks and be a loyal and forever best friend. Ha! That ain't what cats do and he was about to have his notions curtailed and learn that we cats are not domesticated in that way.

Cats get fed. Cats get played with until we tire of the event or the person we are granting the privilege of giving our time to. And if we need to be physically coddled, it is always on our terms, for the amount of time we choose and in a manner that suits our immediate fancy.

I could tell his affection for me was growing rapidly as he watched me play and gently lifted me away from areas where I could easily squeeze my little body through. I managed several times to quickly find my way behind and under things that lead to all these really fun wires and plugs. And while he thought he was rescuing me from harm, I would continually find ways to go back and entangle myself in them, occasionally making the room plunge into darkness.

He seemed genuinely concerned that I would do myself harm if I persisted in finding ways to get to these awesome new playgrounds and he began making things that blocked my passage to them. "This guy is a real killjoy," I kept thinking. "OK. If that's his game, I'll find a new game."

As I began getting more and more familiar with my new environment, my new home, I learned how to get myself up on the higher-level structures in the room.

I worked hard at this. And I energetically ran about playing and making use of everything I could. After all, this was my home and he would just have to bend to what it is like to have and love a cat.

He was far more patient and understanding in the early weeks of our getting to know each other. But as time progressed he could be stubborn about stopping me from certain things I really liked doing. His favorite words seemed to be "no" and "down." I did find a way to make him uneasy, especially after he would chastise me or physically pull me away from something I wanted or wanted to do.

I would sit and stare at him. In particular, I would get up on the coffee table right across from where he was sitting and deep stare at him. Mostly I would stare at his hands.

I *love* his fingers. They would make awesome chew toys or scratching posts. And when he was most unsuspecting I would lunge toward them and play-bite or grab them with my claws. His hands, he feels, are off-limits to my playing. Initially getting on the coffee table at all was firmly off-limits as I hear, "No!", "Down!", "Get off of there." But if I jumped up next to him and dropped my sleepy head on his leg and cuddled into him, if my next move was to the coffee table, he might pretend to not notice. And after several days of repeating this, the coffee table became part of my domain. This was like Caesar conquering all of Gaul as the coffee table was pretty much my only off-limits place in the room. And yes, I do know about Caesar. We cats have ruled supreme since before the days of ancient Egypt where sensible humans revered us as gods. We come embedded with important history that we automatically know from birth.

The hardest things my new keeper has had to learn to contend with are Zoomies. As imperious and dignified as we cats are we also know how to have a good release. We play hard, we sleep long and when the urge is strong we party heartily. Humans think that Zoomies are based on a natural genetic desire to hunt. Yeah, I like to hunt, play at hunting and occasionally actually hunt something down. Just the other day this little flying thing got into the living space and it was zooming about the big window trying to fly through it or something. I get it, sometimes I think I can get through it too. But this flying thing was kind of appetizing so I just kept on it, all over the place, until I actually swatted it down near the window…and ate it. I sat there for an hour hoping one of his friends would come looking for him. Meanwhile, my provider is on the phone with his daughter laughing about it, saying he should have named me Renfield. A few weeks ago he told her he should have named me after another of his literary heroes, Lestat, a vampire - just because I kept biting him. I'm not sure what this Atticus guy he likes did, but I must still be doing that too since he hasn't officially changed my name.

Back to the Zoomies. My provider likes order and logic and I suppose cats are logical creatures for the most part. But when there is an opportunity to party, one should go all out. And that's kind of what the Zoomies are for. Just go wild and release all the tension that builds up. We live in a relatively small environment so the size of my heavy partying moments tends to unnerve my person. But man do I love the adrenaline rush. Sometimes its so great I get a double rush and get a bit aggressive with the hunt issues. My human is the only real moving thing around so I attack. This is probably the only time he just can't find it in his silly heart to love me and he puts me in what he calls "the lockup." Initially the lockup was the grey prison bag I came in. But this is also used when we travel and he doesn't like the idea of it serving a dual purpose that might confuse me. I'm a cat!!!!! I don't get confused no matter what Monty Python thought.

So the bathroom became the lockup until one night – not because the bathroom was being used for the lockup, but just because I felt like it – I clawed and ripped the expensive wallpaper. So it was back to the grey bag no matter how it might confuse me.

Since then he purchased a small dog training crate. He still thinks I can be a dog. This is the new lockup. When I see him taking it out and unfolding it, I know he is really pissed at my behavior. But he's a pushover. He bought a cushy little bed pad to line the bottom with. But because I am a cat I had to show him that that carries no weight with me. First time in the new lockup, I bunched it up and crawled under it. I think he thought I would smother so he let me out and took the pad out and put it away. Now when he uses the lockup it's not there. I may have blown it on that decision.

His friend told him he should buy me a scratch board in addition to the scratching posts that support my kitty-condo that came with me that first day to my forever home. The board came with catnip to be sprinkled on it. I never had it before. I rolled in it and I ate it and it was Zoomies Level II right away. No more catnip for me until I get a bit older when we might - he says "might" - try it out again. Seems on catnip I am what humans refer to as a mean drunk. I was not nice to my human. Oddly he was more concerned that I might have an allergy to the stuff than he was that for almost twenty-four hours, I attacked him every move he made.

But he still loves me. I must really have that Atticus thing he likes for sure. I mean I'm a cat. It's my job to keep him guessing - keep him alert and on the defensive. I am especially pleased then when he goes shopping on Amazon. He is continually intrigued by a book entitled, *How To Know If Your Cat Is Trying To Kill You.* It makes me feel empowered and in control. It's just like the joy I get in knowing that when he is sleeping, my favorite thing to do is to snuggle into the small of his back and feel his warmth. He doesn't know I do this. If he wakes up or turns I'm quick at skedaddling away before he ever knows I was there. He doesn't need to know that I love him back. He needs to know I am a cat and not a dog!

Guarding the Crown Jewels

Like the wallpaper sticks to the wall
Like the seashore clings to the sea
Like you'll never get rid of your shadow
No, you'll never get rid of me
Let all the others fight and fuss
Whatever happens, We've got us

ME AND MY SHADOW
Counterpoint lyrics for
Frank Sinatra & Sammy Davis Jr.
Song by Al Jolsen/Dave Dreyer/Billy Rose

I have no idea why inspiration often takes me to subjects that can only cause me personal embarrassment. Maybe I need to purge myself of hidden guilt or some latent need to face unwarranted fears. But I find myself giving in and unfolding this story against my better judgement. Nonetheless, here goes!

First let me put out an advisory that if mention of genitalia is on your list of subjects that you consider to be in bad taste or might be offensive to your moral standards, perhaps it is best that you allow your sanctified fingers to flip through the remaining pages of this tale and skip straight forward to the next chapter to spare yourself of any unconscious meandering into a situation that would possibly offend the very foundations of your moral fiber.

And if you are one of those readers who upon being told that such a subject matter is forthcoming and you find yourself on the precipice of some titillating submergence into a world of tantalizing kinky eroticism, please, brace yourself for a profound disappointment.

Now that that's cleared up. Let's move forward!

Several months ago I was bequeathed a cute little kitten by my loving daughter. He is truly adorable and the handsomest of cats. Well. He's adorable most of the time. I mean one has to face it - he's a cat. No matter how domesticated we silly human beings think we can make these furry little beasts into docile creatures, truth is, they are instinctively predatory creatures. And they are carnivores. Now while they aren't at all likely to try to snatch the kale out of your healthy garden salad and run off with it, they will, if not strategically trained or left unwatched, they *will* be highly likely to drag the chicken off your dinner plate and scamper off to some hidden spot to celebrate the success of the hunt and their victory in directing you on your way to starvation. They crave flesh. They can't help it. They are just made that way.

Now, because I mentioned "eroticism" earlier, I need to clarify that the kind of flesh craving I am talking about is solely of the food kind here. I have no doubts that cats like any mammal are likely to also have cravings of the carnal nature as well. Sadly for my little guy such amorous entanglements just aren't destined in his stars. He came sans genitalia. I didn't do this to him! But truth be known I would have if the situation were left up to me. But I am not the one who did this to the little guy so technically I am not to blame. Right?

My precious little fur ball companion is very good to me. He does not steal meat or anything, for that matter, from my dinner plate. His taste in food seems happily fulfilled by consuming the most expensive brand of scientifically healthy cat food. Rob me of my food? No. Spend my hard earned money? Yes. Curiously, he is fond of neither fish nor fowl. OK, occasionally he will actually eat the expensive food derived from chicken meat. He will actually clean his bowl. The only surefire meal he will devour is food comprised mostly of red meat. He is a true carnivore. His preference apparently is flesh from mammals. Bless his sweet little heart he will not eat rabbit. I attribute this to the fact that were his ears a little longer and his tail bobbed, he would look like one. And his soft mostly white fur is every bit as soft and cuddly as a bunny rabbit. It is a luxurious pleasure to get to pet him - something only allowed on his terms and on his schedule.

It is flesh he craves. Have I made that clear?

EXTOLLING THE ORDINARY

It has taken me a while to wean him away from his inclinations to try my flesh. My legs arms and hands have areas of small scar tissue from the early days when we were first getting acquainted. In those days, his desire for the smallest taste of me would involve his sinking his sharp claws into me followed by his fangs. I forgive those days since I calculated he knew I was an ardent fan of Anne Rice's *Vampire Chronicles* and he was just trying to impress me with his innate knowledge of that.

Maybe it was just kitten play but I did lose multiple hours of precious sleep in those days worrying that I might be under consideration as a late night snack to fuel his nocturnal prowling and military war tactics being practiced while I slept - or at least tried to sleep. And I thought I was a nocturnal creature! It is normal for cats to stalk and pounce on invisible prey as part of what they do. Purchasing a variety of cat toys, both mechanical and traditional, gave him things to pounce upon and attack. And it seemed to lessen his interest in making me his prey and maybe - I can only say "maybe" - no longer be a thing he might want to eat.

A friend once told me there was only one difference between dogs and cats as pets. And that is that should you die and be cooped up as a corpse for an extended period of time with your beloved dog or cat before you were found, both animals would likely, eventually, eat you for their survival. The difference between a dog and a cat is that the dog would feel sorry afterward.

Being honest about it, I can't help but think that other than his gourmet cat food, I would likely taste far better than his other options of invisible prey or toy mice and fish.

He has gotten good about not attacking my arm if it is dangling off the edge of the bed or over the arm of the sofa. And his feline dreams of becoming a tackle for the NY Giants have also subsided as it is far less often that he will jump out from hiding behind a piece of furniture and spring out, wrapping all four legs around my leg in his feeble attempt to drag me down. He even has stopped clawing me while performing this feat, He knows there will be a penalty on the play if he tries that.

But unable to shake off his being a descendant of the sabertooth tiger he will still upon occasion try to bite my leg before I shake him off. I don't know why he still tries to to make this play as I have yet to lose yardage and I've never lost possession of the ball.

Because I have outwitted him in these matters ninety-five percent of the time when he is calculating the tackle - playful or otherwise - I would think he would just give up. Eventually I imagine he will. But I don't think like a cat, so I must remain ever on my guard when his posture or stare indicates he is totally in his feline world and our cozy little apartment becomes his wild imagined jungle. Mostly he is a lovable little guy but he still has those predatory instincts that will keep me on alert until he becomes the fat lazy cat who sleeps all the time except when I want him to play with a feather stick or sit on my lap and just purr.

I've learned not to pick him up and cuddle him whenever I want the comfort of his affection. He is not a stuffed animal. He, in turn, has learned not to consider me as a meal. Sometimes I will forget and scoop him up to play with him and in return he will conveniently forget that I am not some giant cat treat. Mostly, I don't get a hug and he doesn't get blood. It's a perfect relationship.

I have grown to trust him while I sleep and we have developed a firm understanding about his obsession with my moving fingers or dangling arms. And I feel safe now. At least more than I did when he first arrived. Totality is not a place where I can safely reside.

But something new has started happening. I have a new paranoia of terror. My long-tailed, whiskered buddy follows me everywhere I go - that is as long as I am not wanting him to do so. I like this new affection that he shows. There is something comforting in how our mutual trust and admiration has developed and grown.

I have always been one of those guys who is body-shy in public locker rooms. I have never outgrown that mild fear of exposing my nakedness to the eyes of strangers or even friends. I blame this ill-rooted phobia on my unprotected misguidance of the teachings of the Catholic Church. Being taught to be ashamed of one's nakedness seems an abundant fetish with perversion and overkill about the idea of what may have happened in the Garden of Eden. I am a grown man now and I know my body is not sinful. I just have never escaped the brainwashing of body shaming that misguided Church teachings instilled in me. I continue to work on that.

As a grown man I learned to function normally about this in matters where desired intimacy was on the agenda. But matters driven by the libido have never been forefront in who I am. My appendage has never been something I have been ashamed of - or overly proud of, either, for that matter. Yet truthfully, even writing about this has me blushing with embarrassment that one would expect of a pre-pubescent boy accidentally undressing in a girls locker room. Yet here we are in the middle of a story about my family jewels.

The cat used to run to the farthest accessible part of the apartment whenever I turned the water on in the shower. Cats are not fond of water and my little guy is no exception. Oddly enough he likes sleeping in the bathroom sink - I guess the oval shape of it is somehow soothing to his body - like a simulated ovary in his deserting mother's womb - fond memories of a time before reality set in.

EXTOLLING THE ORDINARY

I have readily learned to relax about my various states of undress before my feline companion. I mean, what's he going to do? Take photos of me and sell them to *The National Enquirer*? Laugh at my scrawny physique? I can be paranoid about such things but in front of a cat? Even my neuroses don't run that deep. I am a grown up…most of the time. My furry roommate and I share the bathroom. His litter box is there so it is as much his territory as it is mine.

Lately my maturing kitten has been sitting in wait for me when I pull back the curtain after a shower. He sits on the sink, which is in immediate proximity to the bathtub. His head is about at my chest level. His paws - also known as claws - are precisely at the level of my genitalia. The little guy sits fascinated at checking out my wet body. It just may be that he wonders how I can be comfortable totally dowsed in water. Likely he is trying to discern how what seemed like a healthy head of hair when I went into the shower now clearly reveals a severely balding pate. It is even possible he is sitting there in anticipation of my throwing the towel over the shower curtain rod to dry because he loves pulling it down. These are all things I tell myself to distract my racing mind from what I really sense is going on.

By the time I finish mostly drying my hair, my trust that any of my previous thoughts are the reasonable motives for my little buddy's fascination is gone. All that evaporates faster than the water on my body as

I notice his intense stare is focused on only one part of my anatomy. Years of overcoming body-shyness paranoia disintegrate and my brain pulsates with what is no longer embarrassment but a panic prompting a mandatory defense of the most sensitive region of my body. Does my penis look like an enlarged thumb to his finger-obsessed nature? And why am I having heightened thinking of his lineage with bobcats and cougars? Does it dangle from my groin as if it were a baby's arm he would like to play with? And worst of all, does my precious little kitty understand exactly what this thing is that hangs between my legs? Does he remember having one of his own and is now growing in justified anger about what was done to him and planning a violent revenge?

He just sits there staring, more and more intently as his eyes are widening and fixating with a growing focus that is rather threatening. His eyes are getting bigger - now they are like alien flying saucers and I can see the death rays being moved to position at the portals, pointing toward the target as his entire body readies for the leap. I quickly drop the towel to waist level and then tie it around my body - protective shields are up and then he leaps!…off the edge of the sink and runs off into the apartment proper. Safe! Thank God! That was…well…way too, too stressful.

As I allow myself to relax, I attribute the event as more of a product of my overactive imagination and my long existing paranoid feelings of exposed nakedness. And I get dressed and forget about it.

Next day. Next shower. Getting out I pull back the curtain and there he is. Same ominous stare. He is twitching a bit with some unknowable anticipation. What is he thinking? What is it that he wants? Maybe it's just a simple case of penis envy. But this would not be just a simple case as there are likely thoughts of vengeance since someone (Not me!) stole his. Perhaps he thinks it comes off and disappears like all the baffling hair loss that occurs while I'm splashing in the downpour behind the curtain. Does he inherently know that this protuberance of flesh is the Achilles heel of every man that walks the planet? And can he deduce that it would be so much easier to take me down this way rather than practicing for a position on the New York Giants?

Mostly, I think he is enjoying the smell of fear he gets coming from my freshly cleaned body. Am I just a cornered mouse he is toying with as we dance this ominous tango day after day? Truth be known, my awareness of my family jewels has not been so forefront in my activities since the last century. Yes, I am that old and have been completely single and celibate since the dawn of the new millennium! All the same I must protect the jewels if for no other reason than for the avoidance of excruciating pain and prevention of a highly embarrassing mutilation. Yet in a twisted sort of way there is something flattering about being observed as a desirable piece of meat, even if only by a small mammal who wants me as a play thing or at worst scenario, a meal. Retraction. No, no, no, no, no! There is no place for twisted romance in this scenario. I am *not* flattered at all. …well maybe, a little? NO!

Certainly I want no entanglement with a pair of claws for any reason whatsoever. So I remain perplexed by the reason of his ferocious fascination and I know to stay on the defensive. There has been no attack to date but the threat remains as the stare downs do re-occur. It has been years since I have had to contend with whatever debilitating issues I may own regarding body issues. It is most bizarre that at this stage of my life I am facing a newly arisen dimension of that phobia I believed was years behind me.

Gratefully the situation is less foreboding as he seems to have adjusted to the reality that "you can look but don't touch." But I still cannot rid myself of the idea that he is contriving an underground plot against me in revenge for the loss of his own genitalia. How many times do I have to say I didn't do it?!

This morning as I was dressing myself and was adjusting the family jewels into my too expensive boxer briefs he came and sat before me with a new version of the mighty stare. What's he thinking now? No, not letting my mind go there! I have to avoid thinking in that way. I can't afford another psychological complex and I have no energy to learn the art of defense against cat burglars.

Maybe I am overreacting. Maybe he isn't planning on absconding with my family jewels at all. I need to adopt that kind of positive thinking. A friend I spoke with about this - one who is all too aware of my occasional bouts with temporary insanity - suggested that the cat does not view my genitalia as mine. Maybe he thinks, in the spirit of our shared household, what's mine is his - really his - and that I am simply protecting his jewels for him. Knowing my friend thinks because of his awareness of the nihility of my sex life that my appendage would proportionally, realistically, be able to be surgically transplanted to my cat, offers a despairingly comfortable escape from the triggers of my current angst on this matter.

Aside from my friend's sarcastic summation of my physical manhood, it does not negate the serious issue at hand - or claw. I know my cat. And I know in time he eventually will take what he believes is his. He does it all the time. And so I can find no comfort. I have no solution but to spend the rest of my days with my feline buddy, constantly on guard, for that moment he decides to make his heist.

Fantasy

Admitted Fantasies

*I know a place where dreams are born
And time is never planned
Its not on any chart
You must find it with your heart
Never Never Land
It might be miles beyond the moon
Or right there where you stand
Just have an open mind
And suddenly you'll find
Never Never Land*

NEVER NEVER LAND
by Jule Styne, Betty Comden
& Adolph Green
from the musical PETER PAN

There is a majesty about lighthouses that deeply intrigues me even to this day. Not all lighthouses are tall but they all render an image of great height. The crowns of powerful lights that top each structure further the godlike presences of these peculiar and important buildings.

Maybe because I have always wished to be taller than I am, I hold them in a twisted awe or envy of their statuesque presences. For certain, I am drawn to them for their locations as landmarks near great bodies of water – usually the ocean.

Oceans are the closest thing to God that I can understand. Oceans are great healers. I don't believe there is anything that is more assured to my feeling better than the intake of ocean air. It has a calming affect on me that somehow transforms my body – physically, mentally and spiritually – to repel whatever is troubling or plaguing me.

In addition to the unique scent of the air, I love the sounds that help sculpt each coastal landscape. Because there is not just one, the auditory dimensions can affect the almost medicinal experience of absorbing the sensory landscapes of just being there. The rhythmic crashing of waves as they reach the shore is a mystical music. Then there is the the contrapuntal swishing gurgle as it finds its way through small and large caverns of rocks that try to obstruct the determination of the flowing waters to reach an awaiting shore. And to unite the elements of this profound concerto is the most special of moments - the quietude, when the tides are at rest – or seem to be – especially in small bays or coves. There seems to be a muffled hum to these lightly rolling waters. God's music is written for the ages.

The call of gulls, the fog horns of ships out on the horizon and the flapping noises of flags or banners planted on shore as the gusts of wind disturb their gentleness – to sing like chants, mixed with the salt air and the magnetic push and pull of the unseen undertow, were made to calm my soul and center and retune by being. These are all valuable gifts presented by the environment of the ocean and it's lighthouses.

Over the years, since childhood, I have collected a vast number of sea shells. They come from beaches of New England, Florida, North Carolina, California, Aruba and the South American island of Tobago. They are collected in a large glass tubular vase that serves as the base of a lamp I own that is topped with a Tiffany glass lampshade depicting the Cape Hatteras Lighthouse. These souvenirs and the image of the Tiffany shade are likely as close to being a lighthouse keeper as I will ever be.

The key aspect of being by the ocean is the awareness of the power it holds. Again, I can only say that it is the closest thing I know to understanding God – the notion of something – almighty.

My admitted obsession with the ocean is that as wondrous and calming and beautiful as it is, it also has the power to frighten. The immensity of its size alone is daunting. It separates continents and peoples and yet also connects and gives life. The contradictory and duplicitous nature of this thing we call the ocean is so mesmerizing and magnetic to me that I am sure it is behind the draw that brought me to wanting to be a lighthouse keeper when I reached the age of retirement. There is a deep logic behind why I would be drawn to these mascots for the all powerful oracle we call the ocean.

Do I really know what the skills of a lighthouse keeper are and the things you need to know how to do to qualify to be one? No, simply no. I do not. And while I did at some point in my amorous period of fantasy, while aspiring to such a lifestyle, investigated, only with the focus of the laziest of poor students, just what it might entail, I never took any dedicated effort of my ambition to do so. It was a fantasy. It was a romantic notion of solitude, living in one of the uniquest of architectural structures throughout the world and basking in the magic of oceanside living. And maybe, if I dig deep into my hidden psychology, in some frightened agnostically conceived idea, I thought it might bring me closer to aligning with some sense of the Divine.

In all likelihood it was some tangled sense of an idea grown in the cyclone of teenage hormones, dreams and fears. I am sure that is all it was.

I reason this because when I was in my mid-teens I thought I had a calling to join the clergy.

I was raised Catholic. And in my formative years the Mass was still said in Latin. It all sounded so pretty and the actual celebration of the Mass on Sunday was an especially sensational physical spectacle to behold. What young child wouldn't be mystified by its magic and lured to it's hidden magic. There were the colorful vestments of the priests that changed with the seasons of the liturgy, the processions of the altar boys, all those gold props of chalices and trays and incense burners and other religious paraphernalia to keep the spectacle of it all wondrous. And amidst the grandeur was the ideology that there was an idea of promoting human kindness behind all this grandiose spectacle.

The unlikely aspect of considering a life in the clergy was probably more of a romantic idea than some power the mystery of faith or a genuine "calling" was dangling before me. I was enthralled with the idea that after basic seminary training I would dedicate my religious life as a Trappist Monk. I think I liked the costume. As I remember, I think the robes were brown with hoods – a kind of St. Francis of Assisi garb. And there was the daily work of nothing but prayer and gardening. Somewhere in my confused teenage adolescence and sense of reason, it is also possible that I may have confused the whole picture with a sublimated desire to play Friar Lawrence in a production of *Romeo and Juliet* someday.

But the most dauntingly off-the-mark thing about this dream, this fantasy I danced with, was the thing that

EXTOLLING THE ORDINARY

drew me most to the Trappists. They took a vow of silence.

Anyone who knows me, even a little, can testify that me keeping my mouth shut or not expressing an opinion is as absurd a request as anyone might conjure. Even all these years later I have to pause and try and deeply reflect to see if I can find an iota of understanding that would make me think this was even minutely possible. My parents were thinking I would likely be a lawyer as my propensity toward arguing was so up front in my character.

In retrospect I confess I was a somewhat sullen youth and prone to much self doubt and embracing a surrender to feelings of inferiority. I was smaller in stature than most guys my age, plagued with acne issues and to be fully honest, not the run of the mill ordinary teenage guy in general. Likely silence was an excuse not to have to explain why what was on my outside did not show what I longed to be within.

The dissolution of this fantasy of living out my life in some quaint cloistered monastery on a hill while Maria Rainer was singing on some far off adjacent hilltop (because she too knew she would eventually jump the wall to live a more productive life) did not come from some sensible self-understanding or admission of my only wanting some MGM movie fantasy version of a religious life, or admitting I had no desire to serve the

Church, but from a horror which haunts me to this day. And that event withered my acceptance of organized religions as part of my life forever.

Saturday mornings I would assist with teaching of the younger children in their religious instruction. The classroom I was assigned was at the far end of the corridor on the first floor of the Catholic school where studies took place. Even though it was the first floor it was elevated from the entrance because the ground surrounding the school was on an uneven plane.

It was the first day of instructions that Fall day. I kept the door to my classroom open in case one or several of the little ones arrived late, got lost or misdirected to a wrong classroom. About five minutes after the starting bell I heard the cries and screams of a little guy coming from the hallway – at the end, near the entrance at the top of the steep stairway to the first floor. I calmed my charges and stepped into the hallway.

A very small boy was on the floor, curled-up into a ball and being kicked toward me like he was a soccer ball in play. He was then foot rolled past me. The striker was an older but large framed nun. While she was kicking and foot-rolling him past me, she was screeching at him that she was making sure that he would never be late for religious instruction classes ever again. When she had lined the whimpering boy in alignment with the entrance door to her classroom she made the child

EXTOLLING THE ORDINARY

sit on the floor outside the room. She then entered the classroom.

I asked a friend who was overseeing the classroom next to mine to watch over my classroom and I went to the young man to see if he was alright. He didn't show signs of any physical destruction. Mostly what he was feeling was deep fear. I imagine he mostly pulled himself across the floor in movements that prevented most of the blows from the nun's black orthopedic oxfords that were volleying him down the hallway like a human kickball. To protect himself, most likely he was flipping himself and crawling in self defense as this twisted sister got her feet under him flipping him with each thrust of her punting.

The little guy was terrified, undoubtedly traumatized. He told me his mother dropped him off and told him to find his place inside. She had another place to get to and was running later than he was for the first bell. Likely he was a confident young child when he entered the building, since his mother falsely assumed he would be safe once inside the building and some kind soul would be there to direct or take him to his fellow classmates.

He kept asking what he had done that was wrong and crying that he wanted his mother.

The little guy had never seen a nun before. And I assume no one had even told him that such creatures existed.

My fertile imagination led me to believe the little tyke believed he was being attacked by a giant rabid penguin. And even if my imagination went overboard, I think he would have been safer if that were the real scenario. The scene reminded me of that painfully brutal moment in the movie, "Whatever Happened to Baby Jane?" when Bette Davis is kicking Joan Crawford when she is trapped on the floor out of her wheelchair. It was a movie I had seen despite its condemned rating from the Catholic Church. So much, I guess of my ever having really been a good Catholic.

I brought the young boy to the pastor who oversaw religious instructions and I told him what I had witnessed. I returned to the students of my class and falsely assured them that everything was alright. "Would I have to tell this lie in Confession?" Before I returned I had told the priest I needed to speak with him about this when instructions were over.

My primary question was why would the nun handle this in such a horrid manner. And in my disbelief, I am sure I projected the bigger question of why was this woman allowed near children - or any Christian of faith? He told me the nun was having "personal problems" and he would speak with her, correct her and overall "take care of it" and that I shouldn't concern myself with it or speak to anyone about what I saw because Sister Barbara (that was her name) needed help and prayers and folks knowing she was ill would only add to her difficulties. At that point Sister Barbara would always be Sister Barbarous to me and my first steps down the path to becoming a defrocked Catholic began. Definitely no Francis of Assisi robe for me! And memories of all the kind nuns who I had known before evaporated in the replaying in my mind of what I had witnessed.

I have had many reflective thoughts about Catholicism and the clergy over the years. Things I observed while I pursued the friendship and guidance of the nuns and priests I knew. Most of them were good people to my knowledge. But I grew more and more aware of a darker mystery to some of these people. My angels kept me alert and over time guided me away from thoughts and dreams of a religious life. And while to this day, I consider myself a self-practicing Christian, my faith in matters of any organized religion is lost forever - prone to deep speculation. And my fantasy of wearing a brown ecclesiastic robe and living in silence has vanished deeper and further into the gloaming than any Brigadoon ever did.

But not lost is my ongoing need to hold a fantasy, separate from the reality that I live. I am happy with my actual life and am fairly certain there is little to nothing about my life that I would do differently if I had the chance to do it over. But the future … there is so much potential and possibility for adventure and imagination.

My current fantasy is to live in a large hollowed out tree in some mystical forest. Yes, maybe I am a little crazy - plagued by experiences, disappointments and longings that have been put in my path. I am keenly aware that as I grow older, my flights of fantasy, while remaining childlike at the foundation, get more complex and less realistic in things I can actually achieve. Because of this, I have a sense that this one may last longer and keep a stronger hold on me as getting close to achieving it appears to be so distant and unattainable.

My newest fantasy is inspired by a copy of a painting I purchased a few years back. It hangs on a wall in my wee studio apartment. It hangs on a wall I face the most in my daily living and working here. I purchased the artwork instantaneously when I stumbled upon it. The first thought triggered in my brain was "wouldn't it be awesome if there was such a place and I could live there – at least escape there - when I choose?" And escaping there is what I do in daydreams when I am tired or weary of the world in which I live. There is a power in art and an expanded imagination takes hold of me when it draws me into its spell.

The painting is saturated in shades of deep green that are inviting and rich in comfort. The focus is that of a thick, wide trunked tree. Perhaps it is an oak. Maybe it is a Sequoia. Green vines swarm from the ground that is abundant in leafy growth and climb and cling to this uncommonly wide giant plant. At the ground base of the tree is a large, doubled-doorway made out of angled wooden slats. I imagine this wood is very heavy and thick. Two small stone slab steps elevate from the ground to the base of the door frame. There is a path of cobbled small flagstone rocks that create a welcoming path to the door. It is lit by the light that shines through a window above the doorway. The pathway is shaggily lined with ferns that hide an undergrowth of other greenery that in places has clawed its way unevenly onto segments of the cobblestone rustic sidewalk.

Above the doorway is an arched window that fans over the rustic door. And a warm yellow light brightly illuminates the half circle, pie shaped windows that have an internal divide of a smaller arch. The bright soft light within shines with equal vibrance from a four paned rectangular window, open-shuttered in the same angled wood style as the door, that is raised and slightly askew from the center mark above the door. Three other windows are viewable – all constructed with the same rustic shutters and quartered window panes. The one around the corner to the left on the side of the tree exhibits an overgrowth of green leafy vines. Angled to the right above, in a position that fails to make an isosceles triangle, another window illuminates with a brightness that equals the fan window above the door. The final visible window is higher to the right and appears unlit as it peers above the thick bough that is semi-veiled by falling blossomless vines – perhaps Spanish moss – and extends out of the painting.

The higher level of the tree is lush with greenery including the mossy vines that dangle from above. I think, well, I would like to believe (and why shouldn't I be allowed to since I entered here in a fantasy) there are additional windows that are there but hidden in the branches that grace and form the umbrella of this arbor edifice.

The world behind, beyond, maybe all around the tree is unseen. There is a mystical foggy glow of warm light. In the haze of the bright particles of light – perhaps fireflies, maybe magic dust, or maybe even tiny woodland fairies shimmer in the air. The source of light may be magical moons shining from a nearby horizon. Maybe there is a lighthouse on that horizon which casts its beacon through ocean fog that drifts to this quiet place. Maybe the light is no more than two bright lanterns, hung from branches to guide the way to this uncommon getaway.

When I allow my mind to fully take me there, I let myself inside this cabin of nature. What I first see when I enter, starts with a grand yet simple welcome-hall when you clear the double-door entryway. There is a rustic fireplace and some simple but very comfortable furniture placed about. A series of eloquent winding stairs lead upward to the myriad of rooms above. There is a library with a comfy armchair and skillfully carved wooden tables. There is a music room, complete with a baby grand piano – the sort that can play itself if one is needing the music of a piano and not feeling focused or skilled

EXTOLLING THE ORDINARY

enough to tickle the ivories oneself. The room has a vast library of music. There is sheet music, vinyl LPs, 45s, old 78 RPMs. There is a high end speaker system connected to every known kind of player. In a special corner there is a horned gramophone, complete with manual crank. The room is acoustically perfect. Further up in the treetop there is a quiet simple bedroom with low soft lighting. Perhaps a handmade crazy quilt adorns the modest bed.

I haven't visited all the rooms so far. It seems I have only adventured in thoughts that venture not too far from what I love in my own life. But there are many more rooms to explore. And I will get there. I have to – it is essential to life – at least my life.

I don't know what there is up there to be shared and learned and experienced. Perhaps that bright beam of light that is igniting the tree really does come from a statuesque lighthouse watching over some peaceful bay. And as I climb higher in my magic tree-house, when I reach the top…

Maybe that God, whose existence I forever question, that I abandoned when heartbreaking violence took place in his house, will be sitting there emanating all the warm light I have ever seen, felt or known. And I will see it shining everywhere and on everyone. And I will achieve the silence I could not vow.

I can hope. Fantasy is hope.

The Spirit of Inanimate Things

> *If you go down to the woods today*
> *You're sure of a big surprise*
> *If you go down to the woods today*
> *You'd better go in disguise*
> *For every bear that ever there was*
> *Will gather there for certain*
> *Because today's the day*
> *The Teddy Bears have their picnic*
>
> TEDDY BEARS PICNIC
> By Jimmy Kennedy and John W. Bratton

Lying at the edge of my solitary bed early one morning on a day when the bright sunshine was yet to face the world, I found comfort in my waking moments in the discovery that my cat had found his way to nestle up against me below the small circular pillow I embrace through the night. "It's nice to feel loved and wanted," I thought to myself. Because of this simple act of affection I knew it was going to be a good day.

My relationship with my cat is much the same as anyone's relationship with a cat. You have fondness for the furry little critters but you know that there is no constant in expecting a reliable return of affection.

EXTOLLING THE ORDINARY

Cats are cats. That is the only way one can describe the phenomenon. So, this morning's gift was especially welcomed and appreciated.

I hold no negative feelings about the ambivalence of my feline friend's affection or often lack thereof. I am forced to remember my own cautious and borderline dismissive sentiments when I was gifted the little guy without a prior consent of acceptance or any expression of wanting to care for a pet at this point in my life. I hold an unscientific notion that the cat could sense my less than enthusiastic energy when initially experiencing his new caretaker.

You don't own a cat. You care for it.

All those thoughts of "I don't want cat hairs all over every piece of furniture or on my clothing when I leave my apartment," "I take precise care of my possessions and this little thing is going to scratch my furniture and knock things over and break them," and a lengthy list of other rational concerns including "I have never really considered myself a cat kind of person," were all there floating on the air between myself and this cat in the moment of first impressions. I unquestionably was taken with the cuteness of the wiry little beast at first sight. And once I held the active yet frail kitten, the softness of his fur was somewhat reason enough to allow my rationale of reasons that this would not be a good idea, to begin to evaporate. My heart was being won and maybe this would not be the marriage made in hell that was front-forward in my mind.

In the year plus that I and this kitten have grown to know each other, there has been a lot of hell to be endured. The scratches and bite marks on my skin I had never know before were plentiful. And the little kitten grew stronger and being a more-assured cat, was more often distant, aloof and impervious to the wonts of my affection or wishes. In kind it would have to be stated that I have not always been patient with kitty's expressions of curiosity and his natural predatory activities in expressing the very nature of being a cat. By this point in time it seemed the level of understanding of each other and the acceptance of each other's shortcomings had finally reached a healthy plateau.

I deeply love this cat. And seemingly, the cat has at least established a degree of trust that allows him to cuddle with me, at least while he thinks I am fast asleep.

On this particular morning the cat did not run away with the sensing of my awakening. And he drew closer to my face to greet me, remaining docile. And he even purred. It was one of those truly quiet and blessed moments life gives us on numerous occasions that often slip by or are taken for granted without registering the deep beauty in such an occurrence. This morning it was fully noted and appreciated. And in that appreciation a childhood memory of a special toy, or better, an acknowledged friend, was remembered.

Most people know the story of *The Velveteen Rabbit*. As a child, I never read this book and was not aware of the story. In fact, I never read it until a few years back when my daughter gave me the book as a gift. This is my only daughter, my only child, the same one who had the keen insight to bequeath to me the self same cat that woke me on this particular morning. She, perhaps more than anyone, knows the secretly guarded sentimental side of my frailest nature.

She knew I would, even though I was now in my sixties, absorb this story with the same innocence and caring as a young child. And she was right.

Because I believe in magic and Santa Claus and angels in my early golden years, it wouldn't strain her estimation of my tastes and soul to give either gift with confidence.

For those who, like me - well into my life - may not know the story of the velveteen rabbit, here is a very brief summary of the 1922 book by Margery Williams. A young boy is given a stuffed rabbit sewn from velveteen as a Christmas present. He likes the toy but favors other toys more. The rabbit is mostly ignored among the more mechanical toys that hold the boy's interest. The oldest toy in the nursery tells the rabbit that he should be patient as mechanical toys break and are discarded. And he also tells him that a toy can become real when given the boy's love. When the boy's favorite toy gets lost, the Nanny places the velveteen rabbit next to the boy in his bed that night to comfort him and the rabbit then becomes the boy's favorite, and thereafter is included in all he does. The boy comes down with scarlet fever and the doctor orders that all of his toys be burned, including the rabbit. So the rabbit now tattered and worn is put out with the rest of the boy's books and toys to be burned in the back of the garden. Saddened to lose his friend forever, the rabbit cries a real tear. When it hits the ground a magic flower grows from which a magical fairy appears. The fairy takes the rabbit to the forest where he is made into a real rabbit. The next spring the rabbit returns to the garden and sees the now recovered young man. The boy sees the rabbit and recognizes the resemblance to his velveteen rabbit.

What I like most about this tale is of course the magic element. And the element of the power of love. And while I *do* like this little book, I am perplexed by it's ending. What makes it a wonderful story is that while the story is filled with the fantastical, it has a very real kind of ending. There is no real happy-ever-after or even a confirmed understanding that there is either loss or gain in the connection between the boy and the rabbit. My experience in deciphering this tale is clearly colored by my own real life *velveteen rabbit.*

EXTOLLING THE ORDINARY

When my brother was born, a friend of my parents gave them a rag doll clown she had made for their new baby, their first born son. I am not fond of giving the names of people in my stories. I respect their privacy and desire to protect their privacy and shield them from what some might consider my amateur writing skills. But I so love the name of this woman, who I actually saw less than a handful of times in my life, that I have to share it. She passed on decades ago but the magic in her name will always linger with me. Her name was Austra Gunther. I think it is magical and because of the doll she created, I have no doubts she may actually have been gifted with dispersing magic.

My brother, it is reported, was somewhat terrified by the toy. So it was placed aside. A year and eleven months later I was born and apparently I was very taken with the doll right away. This is not earth shattering news as throughout most of our lives my brother and I have more often than not held antithetical and opposing opinions and views on things. It seems only in our later years, with the absence of what always united us, our parents, have we found a genuine alignment.

So the clown rag doll became mine. And befittingly yet not creatively the doll was named, Clowny.

He was made of cotton sheeting fabric with an oval head and his eyes and mouth were embroidered to make his face. I have no idea what color his original clown suit and pointed hat were. Over the decades he had cloaks of many colors. This, amidst many aspects of Clowny, give his life biblical significance. Clowny went everywhere with me. He was my imaginary yet very real friend. As an infant I could always trust my Mom to keep him immaculately clean. But through the years he often became worn and dirty. It is safe to say there were times he was just worn out.

Clowny, though, was like Dorian Grey – he could always get younger. Not only did Mom make him a new outfit when his coverings became tattered and torn but she was also an excellent dermatologist. Over the years Clowny would be refurbished numerous times with completely new skin and embroidered facial features. Most often the miraculous rebirth of Clowny would come at Christmas.

From my years as a toddler, well past a time that I should have detached myself from my inanimate friend, I shared all my secret thoughts, my fears, my joys and frustrations with Clowny. I think it is safe to say that Clowny was a sponge for all that oozed from my soul. He was always on my bed until I went to college. If ever I was in need of comfort, that silly rag doll was there. If I couldn't sleep when I was very young I would rub my pointer finger on the pointed top of his hat. Thank goodness his hat was sewn to his head or I'm sure it would have been lost too many numbers of times from the tugging it got.

EXTOLLING THE ORDINARY

My favorite thing I remember is banging heads with him when I was angry or mad at myself for doing something stupid. And I was unquestionably an odd child and did volumes of stupid things I regretted. Also when I couldn't remember something and thought it was stuck in my head and needed dislodging, I would physically bang his head against my forehead repeatedly until I found a sense of calm. It didn't ever hurt - he was just stuffed tightly with cotton. Maybe when he was first made he had sawdust stuffing like the velveteen rabbit but during all the years I used his head to bang loose the sawdust and cobwebs in my own, it was cotton. I loved the way it felt. It was comparable to having a human friend knock some sense into one's self.

By the time I went to college, all my childhood, no, all my life was stored in the fibers of that amazing rag doll. I don't remember ever taking out anger on it. I doubt I would have. I think I knew too well how much I needed the friendship of this clown. I know and I always knew that he wasn't real. But all the love I sweated or spoke into it was.

When I went to college, the age of Clowny reached its end. Mom held onto him, even giving him a new coat of skin and a bright red and white striped outfit. I do remember the last outfit he had when we last shared dreams through the night on the same bed - it was a pale blue color, faded with dirt and the sweat of being held tightly too often. And his hat was losing stitches that held it to his head. And the pointed top of his hat was frayed. Gee. I wonder why?

One day when my daughter was a little more than a year old, Mom brought Clowny to our home and gave him to my daughter, never asking me if I was OK with this. And even though I was, and even liked the idea that my child might now know the magic I found in this simple handmade toy, something inside of me winced that I had no part in the proceedings. But there was great joy in knowing that my daughter would hold and play with this special thing that held my soul deep within the layers and layers of cotton skin buried behind the new and colorful Clowny, the most important and beloved of my childhood possessions.

Clowny wasn't my daughter's favorite play pal. But she had a fondness for him over some of the other stuffed animals she owned, and God knows she was reminded enough times that this was my favorite toy while I was growing up. Not from me - but from my Mom.

When my daughter was around four she took a car trip to North Carolina alone with her Mom and grandparents to visit with my brother.

She and her Mom and the grandparents made the drive without me. I was stage-managing a season at a quaint summer theater in Connecticut and was unable to go. Clowny and another toy, favored by my little one, I think its name was Puff-a-Lump, also set out on the journey. Somewhere at a rest stop, Clowny went missing, unnoticed until the crew had traveled on significantly longer. And he was gone forever. Attempts to find him were made on the return home but there was no success.

There is only one word for it -*GONE*. The phrase, "lost forever" just doesn't ring truthful in me.

It took weeks for the family to tell me. There is something absurd in human thinking that waiting to deliver sad news can soften the blow. It didn't. But I put on a stoic masculine front and saved my sobbing tears for a lengthy private moment on my own. It's the same thing I had to do when I was casually told that our childhood dog had to be put to sleep - the dog I rescued from being taken to the dog pound with the other puppies born under the garage of a family on my paper route when I was eleven years old. I begged to be allowed to bring her home and won the argument. But I wasn't offered the opportunity to say goodbye before the end had come.

I know as an adult that it was just a rag doll, a toy from my intentionally drawn out childhood. But I also know that so much of my soul was in that little thing that it was something real. And because with love I rubbed away the shell and coverings of that silly thing enough times that it's has been absorbed into me as well. Much like dear friends I have lost, something beyond what can be explained transpired between us over all those years - something maybe unreal - but something that because magic exists - was/is real to me.

I have not lost my sense of what that was/is. And more than a quarter of a century has passed.

I don't know if my daughter thought there was a connection between me and my Clowny and the young boy and his velveteen rabbit when she gave me the book in my adult years or if she just knew it was my kind of story for the liking. Maybe she knew my pain better than I gave her credit for. I don't think this kitten snuggling up to me in my waking hour has any connection to the rag doll clown. But I know it is sharing something with me even if he doesn't remember the moment tomorrow when he will likely run away before I catch his affection again. I, not unlike the end of the story of *The Velveteen Rabbit,* am not fully certain of what the connection between *what was* and *what is* might be.

They say cats see things that we humans do not. It is one of a myriad of explanations of why we see cats staring off with great intensity at something we do not see. Theories are they see ghosts. I do not believe in ghosts per se even though years ago when working in an old opera house I twice encountered a vision, that fit the description of the legendary phantom.

The first encounter was with a shaft of bluish light that slowly swept across my path in the aisle of the theater. It went from floor to ceiling and brought with it a radiance of a very cool breeze amidst the sweltering heat of the summer air that filled the non-air-conditioned building. The second time was when we had a small electrical fire in the upper fly loft. As the firemen arrived and moved toward the stage area to put out the fire above our heads, that same shaft column of light was there by the fire, only this time within the light was a faded silhouette of a man in eighteenth century attire - the time period - 1860's - when the opera house was built. It was much like viewing a hologram.

As said, I am not much of a believer in ghosts but I do firmly believe in spirits. While I neither see them nor hear them, my angels, when not the fully human kind, are of the spirit world. Unlike the illusion at the theater, my spirits do not possess drama of that kind or any nature. When I am working as a stage director they may well get a bit dramatic but they never have had the audacity or ego to show themselves.

But back to the cat. In recent weeks I have stumbled upon an interesting and continuing phenomenon regarding my beloved feline companion.

When Atticus, that is the name I bestowed upon him, was at the rescue center, the kind staff had given him a small six-inch teddy bear when he was of-age to be taken from the adopted stepmother he was blessed to be able to suckle with, as she had just had a litter and he was still small enough to join her kittens. When my daughter rescued him to give to me, they gave the bear to Atticus to keep him company. Of course I have kept that bear and always leave it where my furry feline can always find him.

In the months that Atticus has been with me, I have observed him snuggle with the bear, who I have named -"Mr. Bear"- and I have witnessed him wrestle with it, use it as a kick toy, just carry it around in his mouth, try to hide it and recently, even drag and drop Mr. Bear into the water that slowly drained from one of my showers. In short, he cares for this thing and it is somehow important to him.

Recently I was awakened around two thirty A.M. by a variety of loud, then soft, then moderate meowing sounds. And they continued for several minutes. Alarmed that Atticus had gotten himself trapped somewhere in the apartment I began to rise up when I saw him sitting in the middle of the floor with Mr. Bear. When he saw I had woken-up he looked briefly in my direction then walked away, from me, and from Mr. Bear. A bit of time passed as I settled back into attempting sleep. The meowing resumed and keeping my eyes as sneakily shut as possible and making certain not to move, I saw Atticus, back at center floor, addressing Mr. Bear. It was quite a colorful conversation - well…let us say, lecture, as I never heard Mr. Bear return a word.

EXTOLLING THE ORDINARY

As days passed, I would wake each morning and find Mr. Bear, center floor, just lying there unattended. Every morning. Same place. And sometimes in the shadows of my sleeping state I would hear the purrs and squeaks and singing of Atticus' monologue.

As more days passed, Atticus became more courageous about his need to converse and/or lecture Mr. Bear on what he was thinking. In the daylight hours he would pick up Mr. Bear in his teeth and carry him off to a corner where I could not see and start his cat aria of singing to the bear. Sometimes he would feign play and toss him about to get him out of my view and then start the daily communication.

He now does this daily - sometimes twice a day. But as has been the case since the first night I discovered the nocturnal communication, to this very day, in daylight hours, it has become ritual. If Atticus knows I am watching - the verbal communicative action will stop on a dime. He doesn't seem to care anymore if I hear him - he only stops and covers up the events if I can see them together.

I am all kinds of crazy. I admit as I get older the idiosyncratic thoughts I adopt and grow to believe in can get as close to the brink of insanity as one might dare to get.

But I am sorry. I know that Atticus puts his soul into this little tiny toy bear. Cats have a keener sense of things than we humans. And as I watch the surrendering of his quiet moments with his little bear I know this is his spiritual outlet. He is telling his stories and frustrations and plans to the spirit he has created in this inanimate object. And there is nearby, an angel-spirit recording his tales and history upon its wings.

But on a quiet morning with the sun rising, I am comforted waking to my little buddy who I know can see the spirits I cannot. I am now ready to face another day because for at least in these quickly passing moments or in the glowing haze of an extended span of a rich childhood remembered, I am alive and I can think and dream as well when awake as when I sleep. Because in a world where one can, on occasion, feel alone, there are spirits in inanimate friends who will see us through.

A Dichotomy of Longings

I would like to be here
I would like to be there
I would like to be everywhere at once
I know that's a contradiction in terms
And it's a problem, especially when
My body is clearing forty
And my mind is nearing ten

GUIDO'S SONG
from *NINE*
music and Lyrics by Maury Yeston

A longing often comes
To flee the world
Of all the solid things
That anchor me within

To leave behind
the cubicles, the alley ways
And caverns
Made of stone

Transport me far beyond
The tactile world

EXTOLLING THE ORDINARY

Of solid hardened things
Serving questionable purpose

Remove me to wooded grounds
Where giant oaks
With massive girths
Grow skyward

Oh, to meander deep
Into woodland groves
Where scents of oak and pine
Can permeate the air

To build a home -
A respite place
Carved in a giant trunk
Of a grand and mighty oak

With lanterns strung
Amidst the boughs
And branches
Of the limbs

And windows too
To show the light
Of warmth and care
Inside the bark clad shell

I should have been an elf
A gnome

Kevin Thompson

Some spirit of the woods
To live serenely such

The smell of acorns
And drying leaves
Mixed with scents of ferns
And other undergrowth

And to sleep at night
Amidst hooting owls and
Flickering fireflies standing guard
To protect my quiet sleep

It's odd to have such longings
When the city is my home
The place where comfort lies
And I am most myself

Dreams

My All-time Favorite Dream

Stars shining bright above you
Night breezes seem to whisper "I love you"
Birds singing in the sycamore tree
Dream a little dream of me
...
Sweet dreams till sunbeams find you
Sweet dreams that leave all worries behind you
But in your dreams whatever they be
Dream a little dream of me

"Dream A Little Dream of Me"
Music by Fabian Andre & Wilbur Schwandt
Lyrics by Gus Kahn

Freud believed that dreams were a disguised fulfillment of one's repressed wishes. He held that the studying of dreams provided the easiest pathway to understanding the unconscious activities of the mind. A part of me would love to know what he or qualified dream analysts could tell me about my all-time favorite dream I have ever had. As much as my curiosity yearns for a professional interpretation of this dream, my better senses inform me that it is often best to let sleeping dogs lie. I like walking about freely. I have no inclination toward spending my final days in a padded cell.

EXTOLLING THE ORDINARY

I have found my way into a beautiful pastoral park with friendly green benches welcoming me as I saunter along the pristine pathways. It is a bright sunny day with perfect blue skies. Fluffy picturesque white clouds occasionally float by overhead. I eventually seat myself on one of the traditional style green wooden park benches with iron framework. I sit for a while staring across a small field of manicured grass with a few trees. The grass is a perfect shade of springtime green and it subtly offsets the edging of small nondescript colorful flowers that line the side of the pathway between the pavement and the grass.

Pecking about on the lawn before me are birds. There are pigeons, blackbirds and sparrows. I watch as the larger birds intimidate the sparrows as they seek seeds or other food sources hidden in the grass.

I felt sorry for the little sparrows. Having been a small child I understood the precarious nature of pecking orders amidst larger members of one's species and felt I had a genuine empathy of the inner-monologue of the tiny birds as they were overpowered by the nature-gifted larger ones who forced them away.

I had some popcorn with me that I brought with me, fully intending to surrender the entirety to my feathered friends. I sat pondering how to dispense my modest gift so that the smaller birds were not ousted from the lunchtime banquet.

Suddenly a single sparrow hopped over the barrier of flowers onto the pathway. He looked up at me, perhaps imploring a reason as to why I was not surrendering my intended meal delivery. He looked at me intently -almost accusatory. I returned the gaze in his direction with a greater intensity on my part.

I was stunned. This little bird had an 1890's style men's straw hat upon his tiny head. And more to my surprise, tucked under his left wing he held a size appropriate elegant black walking stick with an impressive gold handle. For an elongated moment we just shared an incredulous exchange of visual bemusement.

Eventually the bird's attire seemed most appropriate and normal to me. I offered a few morsels of the popcorn to the ground before him. He ate them. When he finished he looked up at me and tipped his little hat. Thinking I had seen as much fantastical activity as possible, I returned his gesture with a warm sincere smile.

He looked back at me, then to the left and then to the right. When he realized no one else was watching him, he again looked straight at me. As I observed his behavior, I watched as he bent his left wing under his right wing. I have no idea where his walking stick vanished to. But from under his right wing he pulled out a finely crafted hinged miniature leather briefcase. He placed it on the ground and opened it. I couldn't see over the top half to see what was in there.

EXTOLLING THE ORDINARY

He reached into the case and produced a proportionately scaled-down bottle of scotch – Cutty Sark to be exact – green bottle, yellow label. He unscrewed the top, lifted the opened bottle to his little gullet and guzzled all of the contents. Then he packed up and flew away.

Following my stunned cataclysmic shock of what I had witnessed just happening, I settled back and was drowned in deep gales of laughter until I awoke to the real world where the mirth continued with my uncontrollable chuckling for a minimum of a half an hour before I settled down to be able to return to sleep.

Freud Help Me! Where did this dream come from? What does it mean? What does it say about me? No. No. Please *don't* tell me.

Return Visit From A Beloved Friend

> *She's called me again*
> *And I've taken all my old forgotten hopes*
> *Out of the closet to put them on.*
> *I have found my crumbling crown*
> *Lying where I tossed it.*
> *I thought that I had lost it,*
> *But here I am A Tramp Shining.*
>
> A TRAMP SHINING
> words and music by Jimmy Webb

Your arrival was
   well - unexpected
It has been a
   too long absence
That now melts
   into nothingness

As always your arrival
   announced with muted trumpets
Purifies me of
   the boxed emptiness
I have harbored
   and forgotten about

EXTOLLING THE ORDINARY

The unspoken herald
   that precedes the welcome
Is the explanation
   that you will leave again
And the hidden emptiness
   will be put away again

This time
   as in each time
The expansion of
   what is lost grows
And will one day
   No longer fit into that box

But you are here
   and lost comforts
Have been restored
   including new ones
And I feel a
   wholeness too long missing

The elevation of
   my soaring spirit
Radiates in fathomed
   joy and appreciation
For what I thought
   could never be again

The cat is purring
   pressing against me

Kevin Thompson

In the world outside
   telling me I must return
But for now there is
   beauty in your being here

Outside the cat is
   nuzzling the black velvet
Blanket it will eventually
   damage with his behavior
In here I am procrastinating
   putting the darkness back in the box

I so appreciate your visit
   as short as it will be
Why do we remember
   the trespasses of the living
And sanctify the failures
   of those who've left us

You always tell me
   you are leaving
Before the idea of
   your arrival even lands
And so I hold it precious
   that you even come at all

As I awaken to
   the cat that has fled
And reconnect to a
   world less comforting

EXTOLLING THE ORDINARY

I cherish unreal moments
   As if that makes them real

I try to make sense of
   Why I need your brief returns
That elevate and drop me
   like a human yo-yo
And wonder what I will do with the
   darkness when the box gets too small

Lost in "The Emotional Mall of America"
a quiet nightmare with a lesson

Where am I going?
And what will I find?
What's in this grab-bag that I call my mind?
...No matter where I run I meet myself there.
Looking inside me, what do I see?
Anger and hope and doubt
What am I all about?
And where am I going?
You tell me!

Where Am I Going
Music by Cy Coleman & Lyrics
by Dorothy Fields
From the musical SWEET CHARITY

When it felt like love left me irreclaimable, almost two decades ago, I found myself wandering in a giant mega department store of emotions without a clue of what it was I was there to buy. I knew I had a generous gift card to cover the cost of whatever I would want to purchase and walk out into the world with – something - something new in my pocket, in my backpack, my briefcase or my shopping bag - in my possession.

EXTOLLING THE ORDINARY

The trouble with giant warehouse-like stores that offer you possibly everything except for what you've lost, is that it is far too easy to be pacified and taken advantage of by the things you've never had. Especially if you have carte blanche to walk away with anything and everything your little heart has ever thought it desired.

And one must also face the dilemma of how much can I actually carry out of this place on my own without over-burdening myself or dropping or losing things on the way home. And…what if I bring something home and it doesn't fit me? I hate the rigmarole of bringing things back and returning them. And what if it isn't even returnable to start with? What if what I want is too big for me to carry by myself? Do they deliver? Does my gift certificate cover the cost of delivery? How long would I have to wait for it? Does the void that I am shopping to fill need to be filled by a certain date, time, or moment to be validated as mine? Does my situation have an expiration date?

It didn't take long to absorb that there were as many unanswerable questions as there were choices in this emotional warehouse where all was freely at my disposal and mostly as unwanted as a terminal disease.

The primary question remained. Do I stay and search it all and be cut off from the damaged world I was there to rebuild? Should I at least walk out with *something* in my possession? If so, what? Or do I just leave and forfeit the carte blanche, never to have this opportunity to explore and purchase in this abundant place again? Maybe I should just find a bed or a couch in this massive place, curl up, sleep, test all this comfort and seclusion, and just stay in this deceptively idyllic place until some salesperson makes decisions for me or at least tries to connect me to something I might feel solace in. Or maybe even tell me it is time to leave.

I didn't even know if there was some kind of time-limit I was offered as to how long I could just hang about here. Perhaps if I just don't do anything, things will unravel themselves and what will be will be. And everything will be alright. Then again, maybe if I choose this course, I will never get anywhere. Refusing to select a direction or make choices will leave me in the exact same place I found myself in, when I realized I ended up here. How did I get here anyway?

Ah! That is a prime question I should address. The answer is something that my knowing will give me stronger bearings and point me in some direction – any direction - toward what I need or what I may have thought it was that I wanted when I came here. This hopefully might quell the discomfort that the abundance of choices, the wealth of items and things awaiting my decisions regarding this too, too complicated place that I have found myself embroiled within.

EXTOLLING THE ORDINARY

Suddenly without provocation or rationale, I felt what I most needed was to escape this vastly cavernous place. Not knowing what I wanted or needed was growing aggravatingly incongruous for me as I sensed more and more there was nothing here that I desired. And if there was, I certainly didn't know what it might be.

Right now, the task at hand was to find my way out of this sprawling menagerie of vacuous abundance and hope and pray that discovering tempting items on my journey on my way out did not distract me from my intent.

Knowing that the validity of my blank-check option of choosing all or anything from this place would no longer be available once I exited the revolving door that brings folks in and out of this grandiose, ostentatious, over-hyped, mind boggling, super-store of high priced dreams and empty illusions, I knew I would likely never be allowed to return, having shunned the prestigious and generous offer. But I knew once I was outside again, I would still be me. My world would still be shattered but it would remain a world of my making and understanding.

When I reached the revolving door that I knew was the exit, I was taken aback by the allure of its beauty. In that moment I understood how this shimmering work of stained glass and shiny brass framing may have likely lured me to explore this place.

As I made my way toward the door, vibrant in its myriad colors and carefully placed patchwork of shapes, it glowed with the luminance of the bright sunlight on the other side, my pathway to the exit was abruptly blocked by a tall androgynous and faceless security guard. The creature greeted me with a scrutinizing and disdainful look. As he obstructed my path, he extended his hand. It was not a handshake the automaton was offering. The thing was there to reclaim the carte blanche gift certificate I held in my possession, unknowingly obtained when I was transported into this place. I surrendered the document and the cyber-thing expressed a pre-programmed managerial rebuke of my having not deciding to imbibe in any of the smorgasbord of opulence offered me.

It then, at once, cleared my pathway to the outside world that I anticipated being less bright than I would want it, since the sunlight had vanished somewhat from the revolving door. Yet the light from the outside world continued to illuminate the stained glass pieces and cabochons. It was then I remembered it was the brilliance of the turning colored glass panels that led me into this place. Like a windmill of my mind I had been drawn into this place, being pulled into the airflow like Dorothy on her cyclone ride beyond the rainbow. But once on the inside, the fluorescent lighting did not shine with the same promised vision.

Moving between the swirling panels as I exited, I was bathed in a thousand colors of light until they vanished when I stepped into the once again bright beams of sunlight. The outside was as bright as ever. It had not faded as I thought it had. And although maybe not as complete as I once was, I was still me, even if feeling a little diminished without love.

But the sunlight was majestically shining and it was free to me forever. And as my eyes adjusted to the brightness of the day, I saw on the opposite corner of the street my best friend who was standing there with my daughter. They had been looking for me; wondering where I had recklessly wandered off to.

The sunlight glowed around them and amidst the carbon ash of my lovelorn heart, a small spark, growing to a tiny ember, awoke me to an anticipation of new and different loves that would grow and fill the scorched chamber I thought would be empty forever.

As I crossed the street to join them, I turned back to have one last view of the revolving multi-colored glass door. It was gone. The doors, the super-store – all gone. And when I turned forward I was in another place. There was nothing there but a tranquil ocean sparkling in the beautiful sunlight.

form
Feelings

March 15, 2021

A poem celebrating the birth of Lucille Jayne Daly-DeCapua

There is no song for this piece because a new life has no inspiration but itself

When life comes
a gentle scented breeze
warms the quiet air

When life comes
a gazillion flecks of light
brighten quiet eyes

When life comes
a taste of exotic vanilla
livens quiet tongues

When life comes
faint chimes of golden bells
awaken quieted ears

Sun shines through glistening raindrops

Rainbows intersect with billowing clouds

EXTOLLING THE ORDINARY

Rich clean earth grows nutrition and flowers

And stars and comets dance with the planets

Snow dances on the air with fairies

The oceans warm and hug all earthly shores

When life comes
all else stops
giving joyous welcome

The Future
Hope
Kindness
Faith
Purity of Spirit
Knowledge
…and mostly…
Love

Are born with you.
When life comes

On The Other Side of Alone

Sometimes I wonder
Where I've been, who I am, do I fit in
Make believin' is hard alone
Out here on my own
We're always provin' who we are
Always reachin' for that risin' star
To guide me far and shine me home
Out here on my own

OUT HERE ON MY OWN
by Leslie Gore and Michael Gore
from the feature film "Fame"

There is a journey that takes you to places you didn't expect to visit. That journey is one that takes you to a place where you will get lost.

When I found myself stranded in this place I had not planned to visit, I faced my first experience of being alone - totally alone, lost in a land I had no map to orientate me through. My arrival was the result of a minor exile from all I'd ever known, from a place I thought I knew well and planned to spend all my remaining days. I don't assign a name to this actual locale and I most certainly did not want to name it then.

People tend to edit details from experiences so they can fit and adjust their tolerance for these moments of unpleasantness.

The event that brought me here was divorce. At the time my world was unhinged and while I gathered all the flying scattered pieces from the air-bound debris from the explosion, I knew when I stood at the end of the storm, I would not be in the same place I departed from. Yet I was determined to land firmly on my feet and I believed I had succeeded once the new eerie calm surrounded me. The only important factor that I addressed my attention to was dedicating myself to the well being of my daughter, the only child that life would give me. To shield her from the pain and disruption this sad event would cause was my only concern. Her well being became my everything. I didn't have the time to tend to myself. I didn't have a minuscule iota of thought about myself or any damage that occurred to me.

Maybe that was a subconscious attempt at some kind of self protection I created to deny that the new uncharted circumstances I was facing really had anything to do with me. True; part of me felt like a victim but I was too proud or focused on the resilience of my denial to acknowledge and embrace that impulse. My focus went solely to build all protections that my only child might need and to ensure that whatever new direction my life might be forced to take, I would not allow anything to sever the bond I held with the only person I felt I still knew how to love. And if I embraced any act of selfishness it was to hold fast to that bond - the only apparent thing that mattered in my life anymore.

In the months and first few years following the division of my now dysfunctional family, I lived alone. And the child that I only knew increasing love for found it hard to visit or stay with me. As she held onto her wishes to restore what was lost she could not open to the idea of an additional home in her life. This new place I was hoping to establish as a home where we could hold onto what we had always had was outside her capability to accept. My intent did not translate. I understood her difficulty in accepting this new place that was not created through any fault of hers or of anything within her liking. I painfully accepted this and the piercing reality of the difficulty of maneuvering through the landmines of this difficult terrain brought me more aligned with loneliness than being simply alone in this new place I did not understand or want myself.

Acceptance on both our parts provided a strengthening and trust within the bond we fortunately continued to feel. And this foundation did see us through the years to follow. Eventually I vacated that hollow place that failed to become a home for either of us. I accepted that her world required an understanding that home be where it always was. My new state of transience was not her destiny. And I faced the harshness of the losing hand of cards I was dealt and realized my place was to live a solitary life but one in a place that was right for me to achieve my survival and addressing whatever needs might arise for her from that place.

Right or wrong in finding my own place of solace I also abandoned heartfelt notions of creating new traditions and rituals that might bring us closer together in our now separate but parallel lives. I just ditched those notions. After all, it has been said that humans practice rituals and celebrate traditions, simply as a means of preserving things to keep them as they were. God! I so wanted to keep things as they were and hold onto a safety which had already fallen into an irretrievable past. I wanted things the old way. But this was not how they were now or how they would ever be again. The only thing I could take control of was the present and build on hopes for a future that would bring a new reconstructed happiness.

I should have known from all my years of reading and observations of others that no one can care for another effectively when they are not caring for themself. At the time I did not recognize my own frailty in the situation and only sensed that I needed to keep on performing the one role I knew I was good at and could still continue to be good at - that of being the best father possible. In hindsight by pursuing that goal I inadvertently distanced myself even further from myself. I kept smiling and lying to myself and everyone I engaged with that all was perfectly well with me.

As the years moved forward she courageously found her own way and established a world that was of her own making and choosing. And I watched and I was there for her when asked to be. Unknowingly I increasingly built stronger foundations for my world of loneliness. I still had not learned what it was to be simply alone without the attachment of emotional loss.

I missed a lot of her life. And in knowing that, my world of *alone* befriended that cousin of alone known as loneliness. Living with both, over time I learned to understand and distinguish the deep difference between the two. Loneliness often greets me on the street. It is usually when I see a father with his children or most often just with one child. *Loneliness* mostly pays me a call if I allow myself to feel sorry for myself. And I am not very fond of that part of me. Mostly I know and associate with - *alone*.

Alone is not a bad thing. In fact, it is quite a good thing. Once you get to know it and accept it you can control the effect it has on you. Anyone who has the inability to find alone time will tell you how much they crave and long for such an opportunity. Like anything in excess, too much alone time can be a detriment. Usual cousin, loneliness, invites themselves over when there is an extended period of too much alone.

Once you come to terms with your individual relationship with being alone something wonderfully unique can happen. You can enjoy a healthy marriage with yourself.

Most people's lives in this modern complex world do not afford them sufficient time strictly for themselves. Too many people have lives tightly tied to obligations to others or their job or a routine they have set for themselves. Their world is condensed and perhaps over-structured. Often the lack of "me time" manifests itself into a person defining themselves by the external trappings of their life and they unconsciously pacify themselves with narcissism as a poor stand-in for self awareness and care. It is easy to lose sight of who you really are when you are defined by your profession or by some other important person in your life.

I lived as a married person for twenty-seven of my adult years. This requires the sharing of responsibilities and learning to compromise on many issues. And in that time span I held a number of employed positions that required a hefty amount of my daily hours including demands outside the parameters of my work day. I loved my wife and was content to adjust my personal interests in accordance with the promise of working as a team. And pretty much all of the jobs I held were fulfilling and complementary to the life I had chosen to design for myself. In all those years, only one thing *never* infringed upon my comfort to totally be myself. That was raising my daughter. I could always just be myself in that commitment. I love all aspects of childhood and child rearing. I would guess that the reasoning behind this is based on the ongoing nurturing of the child I hold within myself. In caring for my young daughter there was always the outlet to engage with my own child energies and construct creative play that fed my creative needs in my adult life. Whenever I am feeling miserable it can usually be traced back to a lost contact with the child within me. And little else other than observing the purity of children gives me more joy. It was natural for me to shape my destiny from that when my world was shaken. But just like the person who defines themselves by their job or their connection to another human being, I too was doing myself a great disservice. I was lying to myself. This neither was nor could ever be who I really am.

After the divorce, it took more than half the number of years I committed to my married life to re-engage with myself and find out who the person I called myself truly wanted to be. I had to get to know myself and once I was able to own the right to be alone, I became able to rediscover and trust the person who found himself exiled and stranded in the land of the lost. The weight and pain of letting go of my now gone past found its place as mere history and no longer the definition of who I had now become. For years I let the notion of being alone define me as some kind of a failure - what I thought was the failure of my marriage - what I thought was the failure of deciding that the divorce was what would be best for the child I love - the failures I allowed in not seizing opportunities in the past for advancing my career - and the list of failures went on and on and on. I let being alone define me as an outcast, someone not worthy of more, or entitled to the opportunities that change had brought to me. I didn't understand this thing called - alone.

The demons I let take control of me eventually taught me my thoughts were misguided. They tired me out and even tired themselves out. And from the haze of my exhaustion I found the positive side of being alone. It suddenly became the only view. And when I crossed into that place - that understanding - I recognized the only obstacles or opinions I had to conquer were the ones coming from within me.

And in that discovery I gave myself the right to take the time, I mean really take all the time I might need, to get to know me. It was a nascent moment where I recognized that the most important friend I needed, the person who I was always denying access to, was none other than myself. And after decades of feeling like someone less than who I am, I started taking the time to get to know him and found that I really like this person. I like the effort he puts into preserving the child within himself. I love the ideas he has about angels and the intense value he gives to his friends. I like that he fervently believes in God but deplores organized religion. I love that he understands the value of family. I am lifted by the love he harbors for anyone who shows him kindness. And in looking over his entire life to this point he astounds me with the strength and resilience he has continually displayed through each and every challenge that life has given him. He learns from his pain and he absorbs the smallest tokens of joy as though life offered no finer riches or rewards. And I am impressed that he is grateful to be alone amidst a delicately picked group of people he has elected to be his chosen family.

There is a journey that takes you places that you never thought you would visit. It's a journey you have to take by yourself. You are allowed no travel companion. There can be no one to point out the tourist spots or help you navigate your way through winding streets and alleys that seem to lead nowhere. Avenues that often render you lost. There on your own you discover places and find things that speak to you that you never thought could hold your interest. Ideas that speak to you and show you the myriad of all life's offerings. It is an important voyage to one of the best vacation spots ever. There is no returning from this destination. It is found in the plentifully complex caverns of a place called, "Alone." When your visit there is completed you find yourself relaxed and much more whole than you ever were before you went there. You are no longer lost. And you will never be lost again.

And when your journey, your stay there, is finished, you will find yourself existing on the other side of alone. And like Brigadoon, the place you thought you knew as Alone will vanish in a mist and be gone for another hundred years. The place you thought you were lost in no longer exists. But you will understand and live in comfort with the lessons of Alone for all of your lifetime.

Why I Cry

> *Must have gone the long way home*
> *Because I saw the little boy again*
> *He must be ten years old now*
> *Still walks different*
> *Somebody holds his hand*
> *But nobody else can smile that way*
> *Nobody's gonna change my day*
> *Like him*
> *Then fifteen seconds of grace*
> *Fifteen seconds of grace*
>
> FIFTEEN SECONDS OF GRACE
> song by Jane Kelly Williams

I don't cry easily. No. That is not completely true. There are things that force me to suppress my tears. I don't seem to cry from my eyes. I cry from my heart – my soul.

Pain. It is rarely, if ever, pain that triggers my tears. Physical pain never evokes those pesky droplets to gush over my lower eyelids to stain or wash my cheeks. I am blessed with a high tolerance for pain. No matter how intense or sharp physical pain may prey upon my neurological system, the participation of tears just does not physiologically connect to the experience. I don't know if this is normal. I don't particularly care if it is or if it isn't. I never really took the time or interest to decipher that about myself.

Now, there is a different reality when it comes to emotional or psychological pain or distress. That stuff, that brand of discomfort or pain, can and has been known to initiate the activity of my personal waterworks. Yet even this kind of unwanted transgression against my being doesn't necessarily make me cry. An offense or assault upon my character will not destabilize my emotional comfort zone to the point where I am weakened to unravel. That kind of stuff is far more likely to activate my sense of anger and just lead to a disconnect between the offender and myself. My trigger/response system has created a protective shield against any surrendering of my preciously guarded tears.

Had I constructed this narrative as a poem I would have likely described my tears as the holy water of my soul – which I guess they are since I just went ahead and drew that artsy synonym anyhow. In anointing them as such I recognize them as a medicinal nectar afforded me by the angels who guard me. My angels align with me through my feelings so it is inevitable that the emotional mechanism that controls the wellspring of my tears is at least partially under the control of their guidance.

Any emotional or psychological assault on another living creature is likely capable of releasing the restraints of the dam that holds back the hydrants of precipitation within my soul. I have a low tolerance for witnessing abuse or harm of any kind forwarded to fellow living creatures – people – animals – any gentle spirit of life. Such activity can and will surely puncture any basin holding back the flow of the lubricants that care for my eyes that witness or can envision such cruelty.

For this reason I cry at the deaths of friends, family, beautiful animals and strangers whose work or artistry has touched my life.

Over time – many, many years – I have come to learn that the tears I shed for the loss of those I love or care deeply about come from a complex mixture of feelings and perceptions of the world in which I live. It is not strictly or even mostly a fusion of feelings of loss and sorrow. It is generated in the magical amalgamation and awareness of something greater than ourselves that has transpired and that event is also a culmination of energy made of birth, experience, and the electricity of peaceful surrender and letting go of all that is beautiful about life. It is an explosion of all the precious elements of our existence that we think define us. But in that maelstrom of energy, is a brief and fleeting understanding, if only for a moment in time, of something pure and wonderful – it is the inception of "joy."

Because I believe in the gifts of angels – as spirits of guidance in this world, I like to think it is also a moment of catalyst in birthing angels.

EXTOLLING THE ORDINARY

It is "joy" that *always* makes me cry. Every time I rediscover an awareness and understanding of kindness in others, joy explodes again. And I cry. I cry with gasps and a heaving chest pulsating with the heart – not the biological one that pumps the blood that keeps me alive – but the invisible one that works so hard to keep me full of hope for better things.

One's journey through a life formulates one's awareness of how we perceive we fit into this world. I have always sensed – not always with a strength of conviction – that I am different and uniquely my own entity. And I live in a world full of kindred beings whose similarity only exists in their own uniqueness and wonderful differences.

I know most people don't think this way. So what if there is something interestingly off in the metaphysics of my perceptions.

I do not cry from sadness or pain. I cry because joy happens. I am grateful to feel the affects and effects of joy in the way that I do. I do not own this joy. It is not within me. It happens in the world around me – and out there beyond all that – in the smallest and largest miracles and awaiting-adventures and experiences.

And that is why I cry.

Going Out to Sea

There's only one thing left
And that's the one thing that I needed
Most of all
But the freedom that I gained
Is the loss that led me aimless
To the shore
And I'm borne high on these waves
Swept by the wind and alone
Oh sail me away
Carry me back to my home.

SAIL ME AWAY
Music by Elton John
Lyrics by Bernie Taupin
From the musical *LESTAT*

There are words I never thought were mine
There are words I thought I owned
At least enough
To say I have the right to borrow

For all the time I wished to share
The best of me with those I love
The world, the joy, and all I saw
Would keep me young forever

EXTOLLING THE ORDINARY

The hands of clocks in many rooms
Have traveled round and round
Hours and hours gestate to days
And days then turn to years

And memories have filled those years
To hoist a deeper meaning
Of all the days and years
That sail me through my life

In youth I heard that days go slow
When numerous days you've lived
For me the time has buoyed on
While longing just to give

And now each year is jettisoned
With speeding streams of light
Far greater than the sun
That guardian of my life

The rays still streaming from the sky
To nourish all my days
But the years now heavy - they
Erode the shores of all I've grown

Ancient memories no longer hold
And clocks now just rewind
Yet time starts streaming by
As my purpose sails to sea

Kevin Thompson

I used to own the words of love
I used to borrow more
That light that kept me young in life
Somehow stayed behind at shore

And tides bring in and send it out
And understands its hold
It mocks me now and gifts to me
A word to own named "old."

I ask myself "Did I steer this ship
That took me out to sea?"
Or does life just take you on a raft
So far you cannot see

The shores of yesteryears
Or perhaps I'm only drifting
On my ocean's tender waves
To travel me to better shores

A place with quiet ways
A different view
A place of rest
Is this that place called *"old?"*

The Big "D": an essay

Look, how all our dreams came true
See how I've got me
See how you've got you
And through it all just one thing died
A little thing called love
A feeling deep inside

"You and Me (We Wanted It All)"
Words and Music by Carole Bayer Sager
& Peter Allen

A BRIEF INTRO

There is an episode of *Sesame Street* where the Snuffleupagus family undergoes divorce. At the end, after all the considered and gentle education the parents have given their young one, the family walks home together. When they get there they say their goodbyes. As the father leaves, knowing he will see his little one again, the camera closes in on the little one.

This episode of *Sesame Street* never aired. I saw the segment in an historic retrospective of the fifty years the children's program has blessed our televisions. The episode was deemed too traumatic for children. And while I feel the honesty, need and poignancy of the episode are needed to be experienced, I would agree. I don't know how a child would survive watching this. It wouldn't matter if the child had experience with divorce or if he just was being educated that such a thing exists.

Even softened by the guise of puppets experiencing the situation, I doubt any child could not be anything but haunted forever with the deep cutting sadness that was articulated. I don't doubt as much as I know that would be the scenario because I was cut to the quick by seeing it and the lengthy session of tears and pain I experienced, as a divorced man of almost twenty years, proved more than I could handle.

There is no way to quietly educate a child, or maybe even a caring adult, about divorce and all of the shape-shifting faces it shows forever to those who experience it. Just the mention of the word is a very difficult thing for me to hear. Seeing that short excerpt, which, as painful as it was to experience, led me to think it is a work of artistic genius because of how it was presented, and simply because it *does* cut to the quick.

THE ESSAY

My parents got married in the nineteen forties and they stayed married for their entire lives. They were married for sixty years and my dad lived on for another eight years. My marriage lasted a mere twenty seven years. Despite months of therapy surrounding the dissolving of my marriage, I would be a liar not to concede that there are scars that remain with me from the dissolution of nuptial promises. Some of those scars are deeper and more sensitive than others.

The therapist who guided me through my misgivings wisely had no empathy for my sarcasm, my humor which I held as false security to guard my denial, but told me there was no shame in what I still to this day, subconsciously hold as a failure. After months he decided that I had no further need for his help in unraveling the tangled mess that became the doorway to a life I hadn't either intended or was fully welcoming. He said the questions I continued to have would be answered in time and that he was confident that I was more than astutely capable of finding the answers on my own. I suppose his confidence in me was instrumental in grounding my footing as I walked forward into an unknown future of not knowing exactly who I was anymore.

I don't know if he foresaw what collateral damage I was packing in my bag and taking with me or if he definitely knew and understood this is something that everyone who enters the world of the divorced learns to retain.

I am for the most part a decent man. I feel blessed with empathy for others. And when the dark shadows of what I would like to think are ghosts of disappointment spook me regarding my divorce, I am fortunate in having friends and angels to keep me from too much despair. I am an addicted subscriber to deciphering the semantics of where words denote even minuscule differences of intent. I, for example, clearly distinguish between the notions of something being good or being nice. There is a cavernous difference between them to me. And so when I ponder my likeness to one who is decent, I rest comfortably with the honesty of my integrity and comfortably hold confidence in my fairness to others. But included in the meaning of decent is an ideal of a moral uprightness. And here is where I find I falter.

I don't think I have learned to speak to the heart of what divorce means to me. When I express my insights or opinions I become detached and resort to clinical views and overly descriptive statements that disconnect me from the reality of my place in connection with what divorce is. This is a fair example of what I artificially expound - something that I wrote in an early draft of this essay:

Divorce. I suppose this is often a relatively simplistic solution for many couples whose connection and intertwining of lives has reached a fraying point where a once-firm bond has either imploded or exploded to a point of disintegration that is irreparable. For others it is a tense struggle fraught with fighting, arguing, physical and legal battles only comparable with the proportions of emotional and psychological damage done in highly escalated international confrontations of borderline nuclear wars. There is no fair resolution or balance to be achieved in the end.

I imagine most divorces are constructed like the disassembly of a patchwork crazy-quilt assembled with a myriad of elements mixing both the amicable and the aggressive fire-power of a military defense site in a key and important strategic protection zone. There undoubtedly is a multi-helixed scattering of diverse fragments that individualizes each deconstruction of a fervent covenant that has reached needful requirements of disassembling.

More than eighteen years later I still have not found my own truthful words of what about the experience has placed an incarcerating hold on me. All the reasoning and implications and possible situations that lead two people to dissolve a bond, made with sincere and promising intentions becomes - just science - some psychological transcript of misunderstandings, failed connections, disappointments and unfulfilled dreams. I can study them. I can understand them. And the decent guy I so want to be, can empathize with all the sordid details that fueled the F5 tornado that destroyed much of what was in its path of twenty-seven years of building and dreaming. And in the simplest of statements, the storm, while having been built of strong atmospheric elements, eventually just touched down and did what powerful storms are destined to do.

Rummaging through what is salvageable there is something that still remains and even if it is severely damaged, it survives. There is something - a great intangible - that is embedded in the diametric of all the elements that lead to divorce. Unlike the other elements implied by my observations so far, this is the element that is most difficult, or perhaps even impossible to unravel from the union. Unlike all the scientific, psychological or social syndromes hinted upon heretofore, the key element, the rudimentary element of a marriage bond, is the peskiest when it comes to unwinding the mechanics in achieving a complete divorce.

It is a simple word. It has only four letters. To some it is a dirty word. To some it is what stabilizes and comforts us by choice or for some, it is what kidnaps into submission by its lure. It is the most powerful of the catalysts that leads folks to marriage. It is something that one cannot measure or fully understand. It can be exhibited but cannot be seen.

It is the not-so-simple thing known as love. It is often known as the tie that binds us. Even if it appears to no longer be present between the two people deciding upon divorce, like germs around the kitchen or bathroom sink, or on a doorknob, It remains in some form even if unseen or unfelt.

Love has many facets. It is a kind of shapeshifter among emotions. It has a tight bond with just about every other emotion we feel. And when we deny it or try to rid ourselves of it, it tends to hide itself or speak through our other feelings. While we don't know what it is, we do know it is at least partially composed of molecules of possession and manipulation in addition to all the kind and good ingredients we think we know are held in its DNA. Like any disease, you can find the antidote for it and control its hold on you. But like other viruses it continues to live within you.

It can resurface at any time. We welcome its dominance when it brings us the displays of good health. But the variants it can manifest often trigger unwanted outbreaks.

My personal divorce was a bit of a Jackson Pollock painting. There were occasional smatterings of flecks of bold color and dark uneven lines mingled with faded hues. At the time of the proceedings we did all we could to keep it "amicable." It was mostly civil but was not without several flashes of emotional violence. No matter how hard you try to control the situation, divorce is not an easy undertaking. It is even more difficult when one has a child to consider amidst the unraveling. I don't like to think back on that time of my life. When I do, what I see is some gigantic explosion of flammable chemicals. It was there in great luminosity as part of my life and then it was no more than ashes of nothingness, something burnt out in a place I choose not to remember. In short, it simply was what it was.

I am not sparing the readers of this essay all the details of the bloody mess it actually was or of its intended artful resolve - I am withholding them. Firstly, I am not one to air my dirty laundry in public. And there is enough loathsome reality TV available to all who thirst for such poison. Secondly, I would not now or ever wish to rekindle any aspect of that painful time for myself, my former spouse, or anyone who found the heroics to survive the journey of that part of my life with me. Those who might recall it only know what it was to them and no one's version will ever be the complete and honest truth. Only the angels have recorded it as accurately as it could be scribed.

And a third point: All these years later, with the help of a my highly skilled therapist, I no longer have the stamina to relive and rekindle the emotional torment of that time in my life. I can recall too many details of it and have haunting and vivid memories and dreams about it. I do not deny the reality of it. I am not suppressing it. I just choose to keep it all in a place where I can own and properly control its importance and significance to me. I can control whatever cousins or manifestations of love that might attempt to own the entirety of that moment in my history. The story belongs to more than me. But I only know the truth of my experience. I acknowledge it is not the whole story of which I do not know the details of every aspect. Therefore the story is not mine to tell.

What I can share is how I perceive my experience and what I have learned of love and divorce and why divorce is likely the only monster in the story my life. Maybe the good doctor was right and I need to acknowledge that there is no shame in divorce. But even if I cannot label it or define it, there is an emptiness - or some taunting vacuum that lives within me because of it.

I have allowed "love" to keep much of what I held most dear about my now extinguished marriage. Several years ago I could have claimed that that was a long chapter comprised of more than half of my life. That is no longer the case. Adding the before to the after, my bachelorhood long out-distances my days as a married man. My daughter has now lived longer than the number of years of my marriage. Time moves everything forward.

My former wife and I now have a very amiable relationship. There is a genuine caring that we have cultivated as we rebuilt our new version of the construct of family both for and with our only child. It is not anything like the union we once built and then moved away from. Choosing to divorce took that and put the remnants somewhere out there in the universe where we will never see that again. It is recorded on the wings of some angel who no longer visits me with the comfort of old stories. Perhaps the angel shares those tales of all that was good in that time with folks who can benefit and learn from them and keep their life stories void of a chapter that ends with divorce.

I always say I do not cry about things that make me sad. That is not completely true. There are two things I encounter that have the power to crush my heart and wrench my soul, to hurt me deep enough to bring my tears. I do my best to not share those tears. But each time those events shatter me deep within and take a small piece of my life.

The first is a child crying. It does not matter the cause for the crying. The child has fallen. The child is hurt. The child is just tired and out of sorts. Often it is the deep disappointment of not being able to get something of want. That sound lacerates all that holds me together and echoes through my being like the reverberating echo of a cry for help in some enormous canyon. I appear to be hyper-sensitive to that sound which articulates a disparity, something far removed from hope, coming from a place of emptiness longing to be filled.

The other is observing a person, or especially a child, seeking to understand a moment of immediate loss in wrestling with divorce. The word alone rumples all that gives me comfort. Divorce does not cry out for something. It sits quietly, seemingly harmless, posing as an answer to conflict - great or small - and menacingly fails to warn of all the unanswered questions, pain, loss, and most importantly - the mangling of the innocence of love. It reeks more of destruction than solution.

People often walk away from divorce without what I speak of. Or at least they display that. I hope they actually do. But I can't help but think that in quiet, away from everyone, these folks bristle, at least, a little, from the taunts from the demons who are the ghosts of divorce

Little Snuffy doesn't likely have a soul beyond the mechanics of the scenario that the writers of *Sesame Street* crafted. It is important that we know that we are greater than specific events in our lives. It's good to move on, with or without the knowledge that the endings we had hoped for will now be different. But whenever I see people go separate ways after they once bonded with a love that eventually didn't stand a chance against the rest of their lives, events, and situations, I become less whole. And whenever I hear the "D" word, I struggle with what I would like to be able to forget. But mostly, I will always feel whatever that sensation was that emanated from Little Snuffy and his father in that censored episode of Sesame Street.

Withering

> *Every day a little sting*
> *In the heart and in the head*
> *Every move and every breath*
> *And you hardly feel a thing*
> *Brings a perfect little death*
>
> "Every Day A Little Death"
> By Stephen Sondheim
> from the musical *A Little Night Music*

I recall in the days of my distant youth, my parents, my grandmothers, pretty much all of the elders I knew in my formative years, told stories of times lived before I entered the population of this growing and changing world. I sense that for many of my generation, each tale of what used to be was earmarked with the rolling of eyes and a broad comic wincing that would bring forth a silent or actual abrupt verbal outburst of "here we go again" or some paraphrased expression of "Do we have to hear about the old days all the time?"

I was an odd child. I liked these stories. They allowed me to travel in my imagination to a time that seemed different and often better than my own. I would wonder what I would be like in that time and place. Would I like it? Would I wonder about a better future that would lift me from the confines of the time in which I was living? Maybe I wanted to be one of those elders one day and tell my own tales of times gone by.

I am not the tidiest of humans. I crave order in the physical things around me while paradoxically long to not be bound by preconceived notions and formal rules with convoluted reasoning that I cannot grasp. But solidly rooted behind my longing to live an unbound existence, there is an equal desire for cemented foundations that create a structure into which everything can be comfortably housed.

I have learned throughout my years, that much of surviving life is learning to let go. Let go of things. Let go of ideas. And yes, letting go of people. Because of this awareness I have adopted a preciousness about people and things in my life that become increasingly hard to resign into relegating to the past.

Somewhere in the Fibber McGee's closet of things stored in my sometimes muddled brain, I have sensed a gut feeling in matters of letting-go. I am relinquishing too much of the precious few items that give my life some comfort and protection. With my discarding of notions and ideas, I feel I am surrendering days of my longevity while I barter off those notions and ideas in surrendering to demands of the here and now.

I love my life and everything about it - all that stuff that has brought me from the "then" to the "now." So the thought of surrendering time from my longevity is something I cringe about but I can't stop it. And the agitation of loss of things I hold dear, mixed with that, undoubtedly gives a reasonable credibility to my gut feeling that my days may be more numbered than I would like. It's like debilitating medical issues ignite a stress into our lives, it is likely that the winces of emotional disappointment and loss also add to the chemical wearing down of human determination to go on. I feel like I am withering.

I have been awesomely blessed with the gift of wonderful people in my life. Too many were taken from this world at a young age, leaving me bereft of their gifts and support. Throughout the years losing parents, and family also makes for an emptiness I have had to reckon with. My experience has been that losing our parents and grandparents challenges us for certain. But it seems that Life equips us with the fortitude to process such immense losses. I think we intrinsically know how to rehearse and process that severance when the moments are upon us to prepare us for the shock. And we also genetically understand that we carry those people within us as we complete our own lives.

Losing close friends is not something we expect or necessarily are biologically equipped to process. It is unlike the unspoken genetic understanding of our relationships with our parents. I only have one sibling. I don't believe I am programmed to understand that loss should I face that need. An element of equality defines that relationship on different terms.

But I am no stranger to the loss of close friends. I am not referring to the many wonderful people I have been blessed to have intermingled in my life. I speak of a handful of beyond-special people who have graced and shaped my life to the point where they still linger daily in my thoughts. They all were younger than me and left the world and me too soon.

From what I have learned from the accumulated losses of their spirit, I hold a deep awareness of the supreme value of a life and the fragility of words shared and time borrowed. Life has carved an environment for me that has perhaps made me too sensitive.

So I treasure things that others may not. And when those things slowly evaporate from my world, I wither and pine for them as I do for the longing of time and conversation with lost parents and dear, dear friends. I am held steady by the handful of friends who keep me going with their love and humor and acceptance of my individual quirks. And at times, that is all that keeps me going.

As I have grown I have learned to mourn the disappearance of many things - things that gave me great comfort and joy. Things like Gerber's Pablum (I ate it until I went to college and then it was taken off the market - supposedly it had addictive properties or harmful chemicals - but I'm still here). I miss a lot of things that are no longer made or wanted because they were no longer stylish or too old fashioned. I miss daily family meals and Sunday dinners. Yes I know that in some parts of this world, they are still held. But I want the kind that were true gatherings of folk whose greatest moments were being there with loved ones. And no one had to check their cellphone or run off to another event or have to find a television because they were desperate to see the latest installment of their favorite reality (which it never was or will be) TV show. And I miss hearing the stories of the elders, who even though we joked about their value - vanquishing them to antiquity before their time - connected us to a world we needed to know.

Truthfully what I miss is not the actual stories but an aura of what they intended. Most were about celebrations of traditions and ideologies that the elders wanted to preserve because they held meaning for them. And they were told with love in hopes that we younger folks might preserve the ideals they worked and fought for- things like human rights and dignity and the need for etiquette to help keep some civility in daily existence.

I watch the withering of common courtesy exchanged when passing someone on a sidewalk or narrow passageway with a sense of sorrow. You step to the right. It was once common knowledge - now gone. And

EXTOLLING THE ORDINARY

so I wither and die a little bit inside when I am shoved or forced off the curb - or pushed into a building because the practice is lost.

I wilt when I am chastised when holding a door open for someone - especially a woman who considers it an effrontery to her independence instead of a gesture of respect and regard for another human being. And I die a little more when it seems too hard for someone to say a simple "Thank You" when you extend that courtesy to them.

And I wither further when a person lets a door close on another - or me.

Maybe I am some selfish person because I long for the stories of the elders because now I want to be the elder who tells the stories. And I want people to listen to hear of the time in my life when people held doors for others, people said "Thank You" and would never think to let a door slam on a person behind them. I want those Sunday dinners when everyone sat for hours at the table because this was the most fulfilling thing in the week - to spend endless hours with your family because what they had to share and what you had to share with them was more important than anything else in the world.

I want to tell these stories so that these things might be planted to grow again because they deeply matter.

I want to tell these stories…but I wither.

Truth

Before I Trusted Karma

> *How in the world you gonna see*
> *Laughin' at fools like me?*
> *Who on earth do you think you are*
> *A superstar?*
> *Well right you are*
> *Well we all shine on*
> *Like the moon and the stars and the sun*
> *Well we all shine on*
> *Everyone come on*
> *Instant Karma's gonna get you*
> *Gonna knock you off your feet*
> *Better recognize your brothers*
> *Everyone you meet*

INSTANT KARMA
Song by John Lennon & The Plastic Ono Band

Sometimes the angels are reluctantly forced to record tales that ruffle the feathers on their wings. And sometimes seemingly good people do things that are less than angelic. It should be hoped that when such acts are exercised, they eventually are reduced to memories of embarrassment, and we learn to mend our ways.

EXTOLLING THE ORDINARY

We all do things in the course of our lives that we are not necessarily proud of. Sometimes these things come with a sense of pride or personal amusement when we should actually be ashamed, yet we find delight in gloating about having done them. I have a few of those moments and I am going to lay them out for you here. Judge me if you wish. I am opening the can of worms and if it turns out that it's really a pot of snakes and if my honesty gets me bit, I have no one to blame but myself.

As I have grown older and the gift of patience, learned from my father, grows stronger in me, I am less likely to respond and conduct myself in the manner that the short tales that follow will convey. Partly, I have learned that while vengeance is sweet, it also has a horrid aftertaste, worse than most artificially concocted sweeteners. And while the sweetness is just that - sweet - the more lasting taste of guilt, shame or loss of virtue outweighs the fleeting pleasurable reward.

Being more noble and virtuous than I may have been in my younger years, I am loath to set myself up as a judge of bad character and personally issue the sentencing of the punishment based on my biased perceptions. In short, who elected me judge and jury?

When I was younger I would unleash my Wilkinson Sword tongue faster than a lightning bolt to slash at what I would consider an unfair, undeserved or just plain mean statement or action. As we remain ever more vulnerable to the irrational anger and vitriolic violence of unhinged citizens in the world around us my daughter and friends have been quick to muzzle, silence, or put a stopper on my inclinations, reminding me with such real and terrifying statements as, "Don't! You never know if that person has a gun. You could end up dead. That will do you and those who love you no good. Let it Pass."

Most of the time that would suffice. But then there were occasions when my rage and the gift of wit would unbridle themselves and thrust forth with a drawn rapier heralded for the precision it was wont to exercise. Sometimes the sharpness would triumph. Sometimes the arrogance or bullying that engaged my temperament would overstate the cause, and the artistry of my skills would fall flat. Then I would be forced to back off and concede to the power of that which I wished to disarm.

But as I have gotten older - and I am not completely sure that I can say, also wiser – something else stops me. I have an understanding that doesn't give me the sweet satisfaction I once desired for the immediate punishment that I was once eager to dish out. Now, something gives me a lingering satisfaction of the anticipation and knowledge that righteousness will win out in the end. Karma. I believe the universe is a righteous and just one, and the power of the universe will put the proper balance into play when the moment is most penetrating and beneficial. I won't lie. There are times I pray for that "instant karma" that the Beatles sang would get you in the end so that I might be there to relish the moment. But as I have learned I am not the universe's appointed judge in these matters. And whether or not I get to see the thing turned right or it happens beyond my cognizance, what matters is that what is right will befall.

So with that explanation of my late-life conversion into a somewhat better person, I now unfold a few short tales from the ancient days of my wayward youth when I was armed with the mightiest of swords - my rapier wit - and a less kind heart in matters of matching crimes with cruelty.

Once upon a time, not so long ago but long ago enough that it isn't the current time we now live in, I was invited to an event by an actress that I represented. The event was being held in a formal and austere theater in one of the brownstones that houses one of the several elitist theatrical clubs on the very fashionable Gramercy Park. I had been to the other two comparable places via previous invitations and I actually worked at one directing an evening of short pieces to serve as a fundraiser. I was really eager to see and experience the other noted establishment as it was one that I had never been granted entrance to before. The production we were to see was being produced under an Equity

Showcase code. For those not familiar with this level of producing, it is mostly important to know that the performers, while professional and members of the esteemed actors union, are not paid for the use of their talents. The remuneration they receive is the opportunity to have their work seen by members of the casting, representation and producing communities in the NY theater world.

The day before I was to attend a performance my actress called to say she apologized but the venue was requiring that all attendees must wear proper business attire - suits and professional dresses for the female attendees. Most agents don't dress that upscale on a daily basis but certainly for an occasion it was not an outlandish or unheard of request. I assured her it was no problem.

At that time in my life, even wearing a tie was a major discomfort to me but there are times that proper attire has it's place and I was equipped with a fairly expensive suit that I hardly ever got to wear and was happy to don it for the event.

It was an exceptionally warm spring evening and those of us who were invited industry professionals were held outside before being granted admittance. There were roughly a dozen of us. After a brief waiting period a gentleman came to us at the street and informed us that we were not going to be allowed entrance because the event that was being held was now a black tie evening and we were not properly attired. The demeanor of the man who presented himself to us was like the stuffiest of bad-attitude butlers in a royal estate. He was snide, condescending and intentionally rude. He admonished us and addressed us as inferiors.

Not one for class distinction or any other distinction in the value of one living soul over another, I told the gentleman that since I was being turned away I would need to see the actress I represented. I had a bouquet of flowers for her and needed to let her know that my not being in attendance was not of my design and I wished to apologize. The others began to disperse. I turned to them and told them not to go, that we would be seeing the performance.

My actress came out to see me and was very distraught at hearing what was going on. I told her not to be upset but to go in and tell the acting company that contractually they had the right to not perform since the producers were in violation of the special allowance the contract granted for their right to engage the actors, sans remuneration, for their event. I told her to have the deputy of the show inform the producers that they would not perform unless their invited professional guests were admitted. She did so and quickly the Jeeves-from-hell returned flustered and somewhat diminished to tell us to wait a few moments and that we would be accommodated. Which we all did.

When we got inside plain wooden benches had been placed against the back wall of the auditorium. We were told we could sit there. Actually it was a better, although more distant, view of the stage and was less obstructed since the flooring for the audience had no rise.

We were issued programs and quietly talked amongst ourselves getting to know each other and I was thanked by a few for taking the action I did. Many of these folks would never have fit it into their busy schedules to return on another night. I was glad to afford all the actors their desired chance to have their talents seen.

Before the show actually began a rather snooty dowager approached us all scoffing at us saying, "Whatever is your problem, that you could not dress properly for the occasion?" She chuckled and turned to those with her, proud of speaking her very small mind.

Of course no one was told of the change of required attire. Nor were the actors so informed.

I responded, surprising her, "Finances."

She was taken aback. "Finances? Why *whatever* do you mean?"

"Finances. The same as you," I repeated. She exhibited a confused pause looking for an explanation.

"We simply could not afford to rent or purchase your last minute requested formal wear for your event. You can understand that can't you?"

She was stunned and maybe a tiny bit embarrassed that she attempted to lord herself over us to impress her friends. Her friends were counting on her to show her lame wit. "I don't get the connection." She said,

"Finances," I repeated. "We could not afford to buy or rent the proper attire just as *you* clearly have not been able to afford to buy a new formal gown since...when... the 1950's?" Like a very poor man's Margaret Dumont she withered away embarrassed by her outdated attire... and hopefully her arrogance.

It was the 1980s and while we all stifled our laughter feigning respect, her friends laughed uproariously. It was only appropriate as the word, "comedy" was the very essence of what the establishment was named and cited for.

Speaking of mean old ladies...

While riding a crowded subway, a sour faced elderly woman got on the train. There were still seats available but clearly she expected someone to give their seat - she likely wanted one next to the door. While she carried a cane, there was nothing obviously frail about her and she moved steadily with the jutting precision of a taunted cobra head.

People offered her their seat but she flicked her hand at them indicating she was brushing them away. As the train moved onward the car did get to be a bit crowded and then there were no seats. Madame paced about with great balance considering the train was jostling folks about as it moved along the tracks. Her indignation rising at not being entitled to the seat she clearly wanted, she sneakily began hitting people with her cane. She wasn't a very skilled pretender and it grew obvious she was a much better skilled sadist. She was delighted as she smacked people in the ankles and struck others firmly in the legs. She even struck a gentleman squarely between the legs. All of these actions were deliberate yet executed with attempts to hide what she deemed as her right to hold her ground.

I was one of the folks seated near a door. I was not seated in the position she desired. It was a middle aged woman seated across from me near the other door that held the coveted throne. And she paid for it by receiving a few carefully placed cane sticks across her calves.

The car began to thin out as passengers departed in large numbers at the express stop. Madame DeFarge utilized the opportunity to strike as many on the move as she could. In swinging her cane and poking it at folks she lightly grazed my leg at one point. It didn't hurt. This was likely because I wasn't an intended target.

EXTOLLING THE ORDINARY

At this point folks in the car were watching her with the caution one would give to a sniper whose location was identified.

She had now located herself directly in front of me. She stood over me snarling down at me. Maybe she realized I'd been there for a while and couldn't figure out why she hadn't intentionally assaulted me yet. But the train started to slow down as it pulled into the next station. It stopped and the door opened and Madame realized it was her stop and she moved to the door. People's faces began to light up recognizing that safety was seconds away.

But not for Madame. You see I had seen several people unnecessarily inflicted with intentional pain on this particular journey. So, it wasn't exactly an accident of a misplaced foot as mine slid between her and the path to the door.

You can always count on gravity. What rises itself up - will eventually have to come down. And so she did as she tumbled out the door onto the subway platform. She wasn't hurt - at least not physically or seriously. And she got herself up not knowing what caused her to trip.

As the doors closed folks were amused. A few folks caught what I did and looked at me with a "Oh you bad, bad boy - wish I had done that" smile and suppressed laughter.

Now my name does begin with the letter "K" but my name is not Karma. While I could say it was the devil that made me do it, it was not. It was actually the angel I thought I was being that made me do it. My Wilkinson sword tongue was of no use here, so I utilized my avenging-angel sword - my leg. Yes, it was wrong but a bigger part of me was still glad I did it.

And I don't know why so many of my encounters that employ bad behavior involve old ladies. (I really do like old ladies. At least the kind ones. Most of them.)

A few months back I was in the small supermarket in my neighborhood to simply pick up a loaf of bread. Restrictions due to Covid-19 were in full enforcement regarding social distancing at this location. There was a line, not a very long one - maybe eight people or so. I got my bread and joined the line. An elderly woman with a shopping cart placed herself on top of the woman ahead of me in the line and said to me "I was on the line before you I just walked back over to that aisle because I forgot something." Her delivery was ferocious.

The woman ahead, turned and glared at her because the woman rammed her shopping cart into her to force what she determined was her rightful place in line, and said, "You were never on the line before and you struck me with your cart and you previously pushed me out of your way in the back of the store earlier. This man has been on the line behind me since I got here and he is graciously observing the required six feet distancing which you are not."

Uh-oh! Here is one of those cases where my instincts are telling me I need to set this old broad straight. So...

I told the woman who was legitimately in the line ahead of me that it was all right. I would back up another six feet and let this woman go ahead of me. I thanked her for standing up for me, backed up and scowled at the rude woman. And I said to her, "It is the middle of a pandemic. I have nowhere to be on a time schedule. Please go ahead. You must be very important and have some place to be in a hurry. No problem."

Of course in my head I was saying, "I hope whatever food you are taking home, you choke on you old bat!" I admit, I am not always the most gracious of God's creatures. But by my standards I was on good behavior. I left her punishment to Karma.

I had to make a quick stop at the CVS before I headed home and I headed in the opposite direction of her and watched her head down the street.

On my way home I had gained ground on her travel and saw her part way down a cross street on the way. It looked like she was picking things up off the sidewalk. Maybe the bag ripped. Maybe she let it spill. Was this

Karma in action? I didn't go out of my way to go to her to help or to find out.

I was leaving it all up to Karma. I trusted in Karma. Right? That is what I was doing, Right? I have grown, right? After all, my name is Kevin it is not Karma.

Novembers

So don't be afraid of the power of life
Open your eyes to its wonder
Just as your heart should be open to joy
So it must let in the thunder
Sun that you long for is hidden from view
And only the shadows remain
But that's when you see the true beauty of life
When you learn how to welcome the rain
If you learn to embrace all the passion in life
You must learn how to welcome the rain

WELCOME THE RAIN
Lyrics by Marcy Heisler
Music by Zina Goldrich

The brightest sunlit sky
Yields to gray
As clouds merge
Into the diverse elements
That paint this day
Which defines an ending season

The now barren trees
Whose fashion lies
Dry and crisp and brown

EXTOLLING THE ORDINARY

Upon the ground
Covering their feet
Stand stately still in breezes

Each day brings more chill
To the fading warm
Of Indian summer
As we Sagittarians
Whose days bridge the path
To coming winter, grow strong

The courage to mourn
The warmer brighter days
Emboldens us to welcome
The snow, the Holidays
And anniversaries of birth
That define our favorite time

The cold that freezes
Days ahead
Ensures the right
Of snow to fall
And this is how
We remember our Novembers

The Good-bye

How do you say good-bye
When it is time to say it
And you don't want to say it
How do you even try
There are no earthly words
Gentle enough for healing
One broken hearted feeling
How do you say good-bye?

"How Do You Say Goodbye"
By Gary Geld & Peter Odell
from the musical ANGEL

My friend sat there on the small stoop of the small apartment building he has called home for the past quarter century. The building is one of many adjoined apartment buildings that line the mostly quiet block on this street in Astoria.

I wasn't there to read his thoughts as he gazed up and down the street. Perhaps he was just catching a break from the hours and hours of packing he had been attending to for the past several days. Perhaps he was only seeking the last hours of moving air that would soon vanish in the rising heat that was settling in while hours of work still awaited him. Likely, he was reflecting. He was thinking back on years of time spent living his life in this familiar and much loved neighborhood.

For certain, I know that in his reflection of experiences gained since he first moved into the apartment he was now about to vacate in a few days, was the thought - the reminder - that when he arrived to reside at this address, he had hair. It is an inconsequential event that he has gracefully accepted and one that I will never accept as my own pate grows hairless. It is a testament to his courage and depth of character.

Still handsome, he now sported a shaved head that most likely spared him the aggravation of sweaty locks as he and his lovely wife perspired through the heat of the hot August-city days of preparing to uproot their accustomed life for a new adventure in the western area of upstate New York.

There will be family there to provide the comfort and reassurances that he and his wife had hitherto garnered from the abundance of friends that they had made in their years of residing in the nation's largest and most complicated city. Things would be new. And as is always the forethought in making such life decisions, they would, in all likelihood, be much better as they continued to share their happy life together in the months and years ahead.

As my friend looked about the environs he was soon to leave, he saw three young people moving into the building next door. He found a strangeness in this. "It's like they are picking up where I am leaving off," he thought to himself. He shared that thought with me in a text while arranging for me to pick up a generous gifting of his CD collection. And in sharing that thought, I knew how much harder it was for him to leave this part of his life behind.

He had shared the apartment with several roommates over the years. And he also shared it with a girlfriend for a short while. And mostly he shared it with his beloved cat, who he worried about in making the move to the new home. He had deep concerns of how his furry companion of many years would make the transition. But he and his wife will make sure that all goes well. They are deeply kind and considerate people.

And now before him he was witnessing young folks beginning their new adventure as they moved into a realm that nurtured and thwarted his dreams of two-score- plus years in the place that had grown to become one of the most desired neighborhoods in the city of New York. This was the hearth of his new marriage of a few short years.

I am sure there were memories rekindled as he sat there that may have been long forgotten.

EXTOLLING THE ORDINARY

Because by nature, he is and always has been a glass-*more-than*-half-full kind of guy, the majority of memories were joyous and fondly treasured. And of those that may have been less than heartwarming, I am sure he assigned them the respect and understanding they had brought him. But likely found them much easier to let go.

No doubt there were thoughts of how he would comfort his wife through her emotional detachments from her groundings that she would now be letting go. It is likely those thoughts that will help him survive his own winces of pain that will taunt him until the new surroundings become the normal and the composition of a well deserved new life takes hold. He is just that kind of guy.

In his text he said, "The story continues." His reference was to the young folks he was observing. Although unspoken, it was also about his own life. And it is also about the lives of those who are left behind. That is the nature of good-byes.

I texted him back, "The complex simplicity of life. It is all connected and equally elusive." He returned a "like" stamp on that.

I will see my friend in a few days to accept the gift of his CD collection - a generous gift for sure. Alas it is but a minor thing in the comparison of the gift of his friendship and the assurance of knowing he was nearby and that we would see each other often. That will now remain a part of me, more in memory than reality. There is no doubt the friendship will continue and be nurtured. That is what good friends provide even when distance seeks to obstruct the bonds that unite them.

I don't like goodbyes. They are less painful than farewells but nonetheless they are a bit too deeply painful for my comfort. I will do my best to restrain the tears while not holding back on the affection when I see him in a few days. Nothing is forever except great friendships that find a way to last until we are no more. And in some cases, as is likely in this one, they just continue into eternity.

When I return to places where we shared meals and adventures and good times, I will force myself to look around rather than look inward and become remorseful in my reflection. I will look for those young people he saw down the block, who are just starting out or experiencing the wonders that our friendship provided. And my friend will be there even though he is miles and miles away. I can trust in this because in the reflective solitude of my dear friend's own words - "the story continues."

Seasonal Surrender

Garmented in spice and myrrh and mystery
From the other side of the great green sea
Something strange and beautiful has come
Something rare and beautiful has come
Beautiful has come!

BEAUTIFUL HAS COME
Music by David Spangler
Lyrics by Christopher Gore
from the musical *NEFERTITI*

The last of Spring's green leaves
Have turned to brown
And are falling
And because there is a gusty wind
They dance by my window
This sunny morning

Defying gravity
And hitchhiking on the breeze
They rise
As much as they fall
And float by left and right
Reminding me of spirits flying

EXTOLLING THE ORDINARY

It is merriment in action
Before the sadness of demise
Grateful for all they provided
The shade, the oxygen
And the vibrant gift of color
It is time to bid farewell

Making way for holiday joys
And snowflakes, ice and frost
And the muted colors of winter
Their purpose fulfilled
The dancing leaves
Celebrate life

Chadwick Boseman and Judy Holliday

There's a time for us
Someday a time for us
Time together, with time to spare
Time to learn, time to care...
Somehow, someday, somewhere.

SOMEWHERE
Stephen Sondheim & Leonard Bernstein
from *West Side Story*

When I was thirteen years old I had a paper route. I was probably twelve when I first took it on and learned the responsibility of a job and the dependence that people had on receiving the news. At that age I also learned my responsibility as an American to uphold what was right and required in the maintenance of our freedoms granted through the laws of this land of opportunity. I also learned that there are people in the world whose greed and ignorance of humanity and fairness both exist and have the means to infiltrate the process of American government. I learned of racial suppression and financial corruption.

Maybe it was because in the nineteen sixties my life was confronted with a series of losses that were shaping my development. I lost my maternal grandmother. It was my first encounter with losing someone deeply close and important to my life. That year was also the year the assassination of President John F. Kennedy colored my understanding of the world. I had not yet acquired a fully matured mind in matters of politics and the complexity of life in general. And all these events, sometimes quietly, sometimes simmering on the surface, were part of all I engaged in, and they were shaping me and stirring my understanding of the world and constructing a fragility around all I was taught to believe.

My education of the sometimes corrupt side of American politics was imparted to me by a movie broadcast on The Late Show. Promotion of the movie had been happening during the late afternoon broadcast of The Early Show. (Once upon a time this was the kind of programing that television shared with its audience - old movies.)

Because I had an early rise in the morning, I was not allowed to stay up late and watch The Late Show. I don't know why, but something in me provoked me to break from my usual obedience to my parents and I devised my devious plan to stay up late and watch this movie that had taken a kind of magnetic hold on me. My father had a very early rise to get to work so he retired to bed a little after ten each night. My mother stayed up and watched the late news and went to bed between eleven fifteen and eleven thirty. I suppose it depended on what the news and weather were that day, what would determine exactly what her bedtime would be.

The Late Show started at eleven thirty or eleven-forty-five, I don't remember which. So having taken to my bed around the time my father did, I was lying in anticipation to take a blanket and sneak downstairs to the living room where the television was. That evening, at the end of the news broadcast, my plan moved forward. Mom went into her bedroom that was across the upstairs landing. I anxiously withheld enacting my secret escapade until I was confident I could carry out my plan without being caught.

Feeling safe to execute my plan, I descended the stairs with my blanket. Once I stood before the television, I draped it in the blanket and sat before the black and white screen in the make-shift tent I created to camouflage my secret viewing. I turned the television on and lowered the volume as low as possible without muting the TV.

It started. The opening credits displayed the title - *Born Yesterday*. I was drawn to seeing this black and white film because in the preview the female lead had a confrontation with what seemed to be the male lead. It was her understated but piercingly direct projection of the line, "Will you do me a favor Harry?...Drop dead!" Surely there was something else stirring in me to chance the punishment for disobedience to my parents.

I simply had to learn more about this spitfire of defiance. Maybe it was the courage of her delivery that emboldened me to deviate from my obedience to my parents and led me to find myself sitting under a heavy wool blanket watching an old movie on television as one day passed into the next.

When the movie ended I was taken with the sense of American pride in doing what is right in the face of adversity. And I was more impressed with the character who found the courage to educate herself and do what is right.

The actress who played the role of Billie Dawn was Judy Holliday. I clearly became a die hard fan. The mixture of comedy and compassion that she exuded was something I embraced. I'm not sure if she reminded me of my now-gone grandmother, who was far more intelligent than the character of Billie Dawn but taught me kindness and strength in her low key humor and caring. And she also imparted a keen sense of obligation and discerning between right and wrong.

I had to see more from this fabulous woman/actress who had stolen my teenage heart. I would comb the *TV Guide* looking for other movies she may have appeared in than might be shown on television. A few months later I found a showing of *The Solid Gold Cadillac*. There was brought about another forbidden late night in the wool tent with the television and me. And again, I was mesmerized by the determination of the character she portrayed and the magic of her performance.

One June day in 1965, I went to the street corner where I picked up the bundle of newspapers I was charged to deliver. This was a central drop-off point where all the newspapers were left for the delivery boys and girls to retrieve. So the pile of bundles was a few feet high. And the front pages of the bundles were mostly face down. As I lifted the bundle and flipped it over to break the twine that bound the fifty or so copies of the assemblage of printed pages, I was uplifted by a photo in the mid-right column of the front page. It was a picture of Judy Holliday. As I saw the caption for the photo, a strong sadness fell over me. It read, "Actress Judy Holliday Dies of Cancer." She was forty-three years old.

To this day I remain perplexed that I broke into tears. But I did. I guess the wealth of knowledge and understanding of what her performances gave me, swelled a recognition, deserving of that response. I guess I knew why it made me cry but I didn't grasp the certainty of the significance this loss would play in stimulating my political awareness that wouldn't come until many years later.

EXTOLLING THE ORDINARY

As I delivered my newspapers, a few of the folks who regularly waited on their porches for me to bring them the news put out the usual query, "What's in the news today?"

I would respond that the actress Judy Holliday had died. Sadly, most folks did not know who she was. I get it. She wasn't a Marilyn Monroe or a Sophia Loren, or a weekly face on the popular television programs. Regardless of others' disconnect to her achievements, I was, and am to this day, bereft in a void that was made from the loss of her possible further contribution. And that her talents and heart were gone forever.

Born Yesterday was a play before it was a film. I've seen a number of talented actresses portray Billie Dawn. But no matter how good their work, Miss Holliday always comes to mind. And with her or without her, the play still remains my choice as one of, if not *the* greatest, of American plays.

Today news does not come on the printed page. Well, you can get it that way if you choose but you can get that information quicker online. Faster and complete with all the info checking you need to suss out the whole story.

The other source is television - that wondrous invention that led me to my first awakening to political awareness through the magic of Garson Kanin and the wonderful actress, Judy Holliday.

My television was the source of the news this morning. The nostalgic memory of Miss Holliday and a bundled stack of newspapers in a time longer ago than I care to admit, was awoken from the sad news of this day, as I learned of another significant performer's life-departure. And my surrendering of tears came yet again. My discovery that brilliant actor and humanitarian, Chadwick Boseman, had passed. He too was a mere forty-three years old.

When I was thirteen, my incomprehension of a life ending at forty-three was not as profound as it is today at age sixty-nine. Back then the fear was more personal. My parents were about that age. I did not want to face the reality that they were mortal. That certainly colored my thoughts.

But as was with Ms. Holliday, I am not fully certain why the loss of a celebrity I had no personal connection with moved me so deeply. Maybe I undervalue the power of the cinema and the voices of creation that operate there. I am a bit ashamed that this could be the case. I am, after all, a person who has dedicated his life to work in the entertainment industry. But there is no denying that actors and the projects they give life to deeply affect who we are.

Chadwick Boseman had come to my full notice when I saw the film, *The Black Panther*. Very much like my first encounter with Judy Holliday, there was a power and presence in what I saw on the screen that led me to seek out other films he had contributed to. I wanted to know this man. It was a decades later repeat of my fascination with Miss Holliday.

In the wake of George Floyd, Breonna Taylor and the myriad of others whose loss of life drives the energy behind the Black Lives Matter movement, as a white male, I have had cause to continually question and second guess my self-assurance of the absence of any quietly hidden issues I may have that could deny my claim as an anti-racist person. I need to always double check myself in this matter. I can affirm who and what I *want* to be in these matters but claiming unquestionable confidence that I do not transgress is not yet who I am. Knowing our faults and admitting them is how we better ourselves.

It was June 8, 1965 when I read about the loss of Judy Holliday. News was not disseminated as quickly back then as it is now. And a thirteen year old boy's perception of the world defies regular logic. On June 8th headlines were about four Gemini astronauts returning safely back from space, American Marine jet fighters rallied two attacks on a "Red" zone, and a Connecticut (the state where I lived) law banning birth control was deemed unconstitutional by the U.S. Supreme Court in a vote of 7-2.

On this day, August 29, 2020, the news headlines are about the continuing deaths and infections from the virus, Covid 19, and protests seeking revisions of policing methods in this country and the ongoing debates of undoing systemic racism in our too, too divided nation.

At the time, we were 66 days away from a Presidential election that would determine the fate of our nation, both to the world and for those of us at home. And this morning, on an equal par, the sad announcement of the passing of actor Chadwick Boseman became about something bigger than the sad loss of a great actor.

Because he was so young, the library of work he would have compiled is far less than what we could have been enriched with had he lived. The range of subjects and the versatility of his craft to this point speaks volumes to the depth of his artistic abilities. And one does not have to investigate far to uncover the breadth of his social contributions offered by a man of immense compassion and humanity. There is a reason his death evoked my tears and I am moderately comforted that my sense of loss crossed over any sense of racial divide. And in my mind, he stood for something important to this country of ours and to the values I hold dear.

There are virtues in all he dedicated his life to bring to us. And unlike the entertainment industry of my youth, where a story like *Born Yesterday* had to be presented with a quieter voice than the cinema can display today, his voice was and will continue to be heard in the daily events of our lives as well as in the films he made. In *The Black Panther,* Chadwick Boseman, embodied a hope for a future where the value and ideologies of African American culture and ideas might flourish and see full acceptance and integration into the melting pot of America.

I'm not a dedicated action film fan and I do not rush to see superhero movies. *Black Panther* is/was an exception. While just as serendipitously I was lured to disobedience by a spitfire woman in an old black and white film as a teenager, I was lured by the previews of a grandiose culture pictured in the teasers of the *Black Panther* film. And while I have always academically been excited by the culture of African nations and tribes, and pretty much all cultures, the film sparked an exciting personal awareness of what a world where people of color could build rich societies, untethered to the white Euro-American dominance, and their intelligence, ideas, philosophies, science and art could thrive. Mr. Boseman led me through this entertaining but also enlightening tutorial. I hold a level of gratitude for that which cannot be measured. In the film there are important messages of social injustice and a desire to correct those wrongs.

There is not the separation between the artist and their work in our culture as there was in the nineteen sixties of my youth. I applaud actors, directors and writers who align their careers to advocacy for a world of betterment. And I surmise that my personal alignment to those who do, breeds a kind of abstract familiarity.

Unlike the thirteen year old, already confused by life and loss, sitting on a pile of newspapers and feeling an indescribable loss, I am today fully aware of why I cried this morning at the passing of Chadwick Boseman. I will always cheer-on the outsider, the heroes who break glass ceilings, who find in their lives a way to make this world a better place. There is power in their survival and voice. Whether that survival is a defiance on both sides of midnight, under a heavy wool blanket, or if it is the admiration and fandom of an actor, *any* actor, who enlightens us. I am defenseless against the tears and sorrow when a loss prevents further passing of the virtue of their art to me.

I know why I cry and I know why I am moved to a state where sadness and joy intermingle in the questions and answers of finding my way to be the best that I can be. My falling tears are a statement of joy for what has been given to me. They also fall for a void that exists because the ones who have lifted me are no longer there.

I am not, per se, the kind of individual who is enthralled or enamored with the idea of super-heroes. The real heroes in my life are everyday people who do everyday tasks that touch or better the lives of simple everyday people. Do I know why my life was altered by this man? I do. I can separate the actor from the character and I can separate the actor from the man. The magic of an actor's performance is given life by the spirit of the individual who generates it from within themself. There was something in the enchantment that Mr. Boseman put forth in his films that transcends performance and resonates with a grace rooted in the hope and understanding of what is needed to acquire a better world - a better life.

Three days had passed since I was prompted to write this story and I first heard of the passing of Chadwick Boseman. The ache I get as his name is mentioned and the reiteration of his civic and social contributions are reviewed, there is a growth that surpasses his notoriety as the actor of *Thurman, 42*, his portrayal as James Brown and the iconic role as the King of Wakanda, the African utopia, and it vibrates beyond the movies into a hope for reality. There are still tears. A visual powerhouse hit me hardest when I saw the photo of a young man, a small child, who assembled all of his Marvel action figures standing in a circle around the prone Black Panther figure in the center. The child sat outside the circle, arms folded across his chest - the salute for "Wakanda forever!" The sense of loss - loss of opportunity - and a wealth of what could have been - were taken from both the child and us all. The king is dead, long live the king.

I often write about the child inside of me. That part of me is what attunes me to what is the best and purest of humanity. The image of this particular child with his action figures - which through play gives him hope and launches his dreams and prayers for his own future - is with me forever. The heart of childhood and the longing for a just world is in the essence of childhood and it is our duty to preserve and hold onto that part of ourselves even when the day to day responsibilities of adulthood are thrust upon us.

Somehow I feel aligned with that young boy, working through his grief with his action figures. The situation is not that far from that of a thirteen year old boy in the nineteen sixties feeling the loss of inspiration.

Whether it is Chadwick Bozeman or the roles he played that inspire us; whether it is Judy Holliday or Billie Dawn who touched my soul to believe in the power of Democracy, it is all one and the same. When we feel loss we also gain increased power of hope. When those we have lost remain with us, it continues to inspire us.

I say, "Wakanda forever!" And for anyone who doubts the power and sanctity of Democracy and our need to learn all we can to protect it, improve upon it and understand its fragility, let us unite with the hope of a better world - a more inclusive world. Whether the voice of inspiration comes from our fellow brothers and sisters of color or the late Judy Holliday (an actress in a role that showed us that it is often the voice of women that speak the truest), we should all remain grateful. And if you need clarification on the importance of these ideas because you get lost in political debates that elude our obligation to preserve Democracy or you think it is easy to blur the line between what is right or wrong, I relay the impeccable and timeless delivery of that final line, delivered by Miss Holliday, from the *Born Yesterday* film, "Look it up!"

Where I Live

> *Maybe there's a way for me to go back*
> *Now that I have some direction*
> *It sure would be nice to be back home*
> *Where there is love and affection*
> *And just maybe I can convince time to slow up*
> *Giving me enough time*
> *In my life to grow up*
> *Time be my friend*
> *Let me start again*
>
> HOME
> by Charles Emanuel Smalls
> from *The Wiz*

I live a very large and very tiny life.

When people ask me where I live, I have a number of pat and simplistic answers which I give in a response to convey the expected kind of answer a person is likely seeking. "I live in New York." "I live down this street." "I live in the building with the wine colored canopy at the entrance - near the end of the block." There are a myriad of answers that I give depending on who is asking, where I am standing and what my guess-timation is as to why this is being inquired of me.

EXTOLLING THE ORDINARY

I am, for the most part, a very private person. There are patterns of tests one is required to surmount to acquire admission to my inner circle of restricted compatriots. Depending on my comfort level with an individual, one might get either a detailed or abbreviated answer. We all do this in our daily lives. I will admit to being on the higher end of the snob scale in my execution of such ritual behavior. But I feel it safe to acknowledge that we all conduct ourselves with varying degrees of similar practices and exercises.

Where I live is a private matter. It is perhaps a dangerous thing to not be more forthcoming with the detailed basic facts of my address. "What if I got amnesia or a form of dementia when I no longer recalled the details of the place of safety that I call home." A dear dear friend of mind lived through such an ordeal and wandered the streets of our nation's capital, where she lived for several days before it was noticed that she was somehow disoriented and unable to find her way home. Samaritan police officers had the insight to engage with her and discovered (in her purse - which thank God she had not lost in her wandering) where her dwelling was and took her there. It is reported once she was there her recall fell back into place. Whether this was due to some recognition of the location and her personal artifacts or if it was a subsiding of the disease that was plaguing her and eventually took her life is not a certainty. But one's home can spark a memory.

An abstracted reality is that once she arrived there, this was no longer her home - the place where she lived - where her essence and soul were comforted and cared for by familiar and cherished surroundings. This structure with her belongings was not where she was living. Because of her ailment, the unpaid bills, squalor, and the deterioration of a successful life built here actually no longer gave her a place of residence. I imagine, no-one knew where she was residing inside her mind.

Like her very life, the life I eventually lost from her being taken by this infliction, she was no longer there, defined by what I knew about her. Her residence became no more than a beautiful urban DC townhouse - no longer the place where she truly lived. Her history, her personal accumulation of objects and events were void of a connection to who she was and who she became. Several items from the collection of what defined where she lived and who she was, now reside with me - a bequeathment I treasure and hold with me now - where *I* live.

The space that frames where I live is small - by most observations it is considered tiny. It is a small studio apartment of not much more than four hundred and seventy five square feet. It is not an easy place to store and cherish the physical objects of accumulation of an almost septuagenarian lifetime. But in that aspect it is quite large - huge in my estimation. This is *a* description of where I live.

EXTOLLING THE ORDINARY

I have resided in many different places throughout my years of living on this planet. Every one of those geographic locales has filled the definition of where I live.

My current shelter from the world outside is given life by an over-accumulation of too much furniture for such a small space - a simple bed to rest upon, bookcases filled with books, music, CDs and records and crowded walls of artwork. Table tops, too, give rest to smaller three dimensional objects I consider art.

The walls are filled with paintings and photographs and a duo of handmade quilts, both hung from the same rod near the ceiling, one hidden behind the other and crafted by my DC friend, no longer with us.

All of these things come from a wellspring that broke open early in my life. I am a collector. This collection of things that now surround me to give me comfort and give a kind of tangible meaning to the years of my life, have been gathered into my life because of inspirations given to me by a few special people. Undoubtedly high on that list would be my mother who instilled in me a proclivity for sentimentality and a deep awareness of gratitude for gifts given to me. If someone gave me something, it is likely that I still have it in my possession. There are items from as far back as sixty-five years ago. I can tell you who gave it to me and what the occasion was. The acceptance of a gift has the weight of sacredness to me because of a value instilled in me by my mother. And she too is most responsible for my holding on to items for decades because of the respect she instructed me to recognize in the personal kindness behind whatever was bestowed upon me - they become something beyond mere sentimentality - they acquire state of meaning - something that I do not yet know a word to describe the spiritual importance of attachment.

There are artworks upon my wall created by my now fully grown daughter when she was in kindergarten or preschool that I value with the same intensity as the paintings that I paid hundreds or thousands (yes, I once took that plunge) of dollars for. My attachment to her finger-painted masterpiece of submarine life or the crayon sketched whale she created are regarded as much for the level of artistry in their creation as the heart warming anchoring of memories of her spirit at that young age. That is part of what art is. It is the merging of the soul with the object encapsulated by the artist's hand and eye.

My interest in art - the masters and basically any art piece - can be traced back to an extraordinary grade school teacher who took her responsibility of being a teacher beyond the basics of the public school curriculum. It was a blessing to experience a teacher who went beyond providing the basics of what was required of her to teach. And it was a deeper grace that she revered the arts - all of them important to what I consider a good education.

Art class was not always crayons, watercolors, papier-mache, or holiday crafts and ideas. In the the year I was fortunate to have spent in her classroom, we were shown Van Gogh's *Sunflowers* and learned as much about the artist as was legal for a nine year old in 1950s America.

We were taught who Leonardo DaVinci was and introduced to his *Mona Lisa* - as a masterpiece of world art by a genius who held many accomplishments of brilliance. And we were shown Edward Hopper's famous lighthouse painting. Learning about these works of art and their creators sparked a further interest in me to learn more. And with my mother's assistance I tracked down the company that made the little four inch square prints that we were given for our studies and pasted into our composition notebooks. And for years I ordered similar prints - they only cost pennies - and self-furthered my exploration of artists and their works.

Miss D, our teacher, did not limit our exposure to the arts to only the field of visual arts. But her care in leading exploration of numerous social and cultural areas also contributed to my knowing how to play chess and knowing what grosgrain ribbon is. (I'm not sure exactly when this insight was taught, but my foggy memory recalls making felt door knob covers that were tied on by ribbon laced through holes around the perimeter. I remember her explaining that grosgrain ribbon was heartier and did not fray and break as easily as other ribbons would. Odd to remember that - but I do.)

Music class was not just about learning and singing songs. We would have music class where we would put our heads down on our desk and listen to all kinds and styles of music. I particularly remember hearing *Finlandia,* the Sebelius opus, and Gershwin's *Rhapsody in Blue* for the first time under her tutelage. I am sure there were others that time is hiding from me but what she most intensely awakened me to was the music of the American musical theater.

I had no knowing at that time that this music would shape and define my life. But I did know that I loved it. Storytelling in song that wasn't children's songs - boy! did that awaken something in me that would last forever. Broadway had a good year the year we were privileged to be in Miss D's class. She played the original cast album of *The Sound of Music.* And I learned who Mary Martin was beyond being the TV star of NBC's televised version of the musical *Peter Pan.* Miss D played songs from *West Side Story, Camelot* and *Flower Drum Song* that year. And while it would still be a few years before I would ever see a professional live theater production, a seed was planted that would become a calling and a path to a career chosen outside the norm for an awkward young boy from a factory mill town.

My obsession in learning all I could about the music of the American theater has continued throughout my entire life. Fortunate to be the child of a woman who worked in the radio business for a chain of stations that only played pop music and the Billboard top hits, I was freely given the recordings of musicals that the various labels sent as promotion copies to all the nation's radio stations. They would have ended up in trash bins had I not wanted them. In my youth, the songs of Broadway were on many occasions in the top forty and in those cases recordings would not come my way. Maybe the last one withheld was the recording of *Hair,* which launched more than one hit song. And for about a ten year period of my life, the major portion of my allowance money, my paper route and meager paychecks from early part-time jobs were spent on devouring every original cast album I could get access to.

I think one of the saddest things about being very young, and perhaps the very nature of growing up, is that years go by before it fully dawns on one's self that you finally recognize the importance of certain people and their influence on your life. I have had quite a few extraordinary teachers in my lifetime - at least enough to not exceed counting on one hand those who truly shaped me as a person. There was a high school English teacher who sparked my love of reading, and more importantly, my reading books that initially appeared not to be in my line of interest. There was a religion professor in college who clarified my connection with my Christian upbringing and helped me uncover exactly what my beliefs were, separate from the hocus pocus of the organized fraudulence of the sect I was coached in as a child. And there was my noted mentor teacher who by some special gift of magic energized the work of the rest of my great teachers by coaching me to discover my potential and capacity for further learning. And to simplify to the extreme - she re-emphasized my passion for reading as much as possible about things that held my interest. But mostly, she taught me to believe in myself.

In retrospect, I can now see the power of, and am humbled by the gifts bestowed on me by, these super-heroes of education and in my gratitude, I see them in all the objects that surround me where I live. And as I look around me, and view all the objects of paintings, music, books and recordings, and crafts and games that fill my home, I see the handiwork of my fourth grade teacher, Miss D, who planted the seeds for this jungle of art and ideas that surround me, from a time when she was just starting out as an educator of young people.

Where do I live? As Thornton Wilder might want me to reply: "I live in a studio apartment in Forest Hills, Queens, NYC, New York, USA, on the continent of North America. in the Western Hemisphere of the planet Earth, in the solar system centered by the sun called Sol, in the Milky Way Galaxy…" But in truth… I live somewhere in the shade of objects and ideas grown from knowledge shared and imparted to me by my mother and the wonderful magical teachers, gifts from friends and family, but mostly in the flashing bursts of an enchanted life provided to me by a special woman - Miss D - who planted the seeds that cultivated the arts into my life. For that, the sincerest reply of "Thank You" will never be enough.

"Broad Stripes and Bright Stars"

O Beautiful for heroes proved
In liberating strife,
Who more than self their country love
And mercy more than life!
America, America!
May God thy gold refine
Till all success be nobleness.
And every grain Divine!

AMERICA THE BEAUTIFUL
Lyrics by Kathryn Lee Bates
Music by Samuel A. Ward

January 20, 2021

I awoke this morning to the sight of snow falling outside my window. Snow has always been a comfort to me. As a child, the promise of a thrilling sled ride down the steep sloping hill, which was and is the street on which my childhood years were spent, was ignited by the sight of falling snow. In my teenage years it meant the New England ski slopes were getting blessed with a new blanket of white slippery dust that afforded the inclines and trails with the magic that makes swooshing and gliding down the side of a mountain such a thrilling experience. And the dancing of snowflakes in the air to this day evokes that rush of childhood joy that comes from the proclamation of every child's prayed for glorious phrase, "No school."

My college years, particularly those spent during my undergraduate years on the picturesque campus of Ohio's Denison University, created memorable photographic images of a white blanketed environment, already blessed with its own beauty. The brick sidewalks, the towering chapel building reaching heavenward toward the blurred grey sky, the small white stoned observatory almost camouflaged in the white filled air, the stark contrast of the black lollipop clock that marked the start of the walkway to the eastern side of the campus, and the hillsides and residential quads glistening in the painted strokes of nature's white, all lasting memories of a much loved time in my life. And the most vivid pictures seem to be of images with snow falling on one of the last hills in America's Midwest before the land goes flat. Snowfall always seemed to glisten, enhancing what was already deemed to be one of the most beautiful college campuses in the country.

In addition to the beauty with which it adorned the landscape, it also brought with it a deeply astounding surrounding quiet. Not only were the buildings and grounds gently wrapped in a pristine white, but the very air around everything was silenced - at least muffled - to a degree of almost vacuum-like quietude.

It was from these treasured moments that my submission to the spellbinding rhapsody of the power of snow's more lyrical nature came to shape the absorption of my affinity for the grace of every snowfall. For me there is an immediate sensation of sanctuary and a connection to the Divine that is derived from the solemnity of falling snow. It presents a visualization of spiritual comfort - a universe of galaxies birthing serenity. The world seems neutralized and all is clean for new beginnings. Time stands still within the gliding downpour of uniquely singular droplets of frozen precipitation. I surmise it evokes a kind of self cleansing of my mind as well.

And this is how my day began on this, the twentieth day of January 2021. The preceding days alerted me to the understanding that this was to be an historic day for our nation. It had been a tumultuous and frightening couple of weeks leading to the dawning of this new day. There was lingering uncertainty if the smoldering ashes of the assault on the democratic foundations of our government would bring new flames of violence. But it snowed where I was this morning and I felt confident this day would be clean of the lies and false unwarranted claims of faux-patriotism from those who conceal their racism in mangled symbols and statements under the pretense of "making America great again (again.)" Snow brings the promise of the new. And today would not be a day for the cowards who lack the simple bravery of stating what they truly stand for.

EXTOLLING THE ORDINARY

Snow falling was the symbolic voice answering a séance I had not initiated but seemed to have been invited to join. I took it as a sign of peace from the powers of the universe that things would go well on this day.

Having turned on my television to launch the day, in anticipation of watching the pageantry of new power in the government, I saw from the various channels I scanned that it was a bright and sunny day in our nation's capital. The bright beams illuminated the Capitol building showing no diminishing of luster from the demolition and trespassing of the earlier weeks.

The snow that filled the air outside my window carried on for a couple of hours, amounting to no significant accumulation but continuing to paint the wind with its promise of serenity. Then it stopped and the same sunshine I witnessed reigning down on the festivities in preparation in Washington D.C. broke through the clouds and illuminated the world immediately outside my window.

Viewing my television screen, I half heartedly listened to the reporters accounts of the activities of the preparation for the ceremony to take place a few hours from now. I put more focus on the prepariation of my morning breakfast. Eventually, settling in with my prepared meal, I awaited the actual start of the ceremony. I was quelled of any angst I may have been suppressing as I viewed the relative calm of the scenes being shown by the reporters and by the anointment of my morning snow.

There was an almost unremembered sense of happiness as I thought of the country with new beginnings. I understood there would be no magical instantaneous restoration of the somewhat saner world I recalled from the very distant four years previous. But new vestiges of hope were releasing me from the extreme uneasiness, discomfort and fear that had continuously wore me down over the four years that weighed on me like a century of hard living.

The event happened and I watched it all on my flat screen. Firstly I was taken with the joy that pervaded the civility and formality of the occasion. There were words of hope and promise, and while not in equal balance, they were delivered by people on both sides of the political aisle. Tradition, and the pomp and circumstance of occasions such as this, serve as anchors and symbols that our democracy is safely anchored in a protected harbor. Because of the times -(Covid and insurrection protection)- there were elements and traditions usually in the forefront that were not present in this particular transfer of leadership. I for one felt no particular sense of loss as they were omitted for the more important thing - that of the event prevailing.

EXTOLLING THE ORDINARY

The excitement of the installation of the first female vice president is cause for jubilation. There may have been no giant crowd on the National Mall to cheer this much-needed coming of age for our nation but the rejoicing across the country for this momentous occasion could be felt, even outside the very window that revealed the snow and sun at the start of my day.

And…THERE WAS SNOW! The sunshine in DC gave way to a light sprinkling as guests and leaders made their way from inside the Capitol onto the seating arranged on the West Wing stairs and gathering areas. It was heaven christening serenity on those who will lead us in the days to come.

The new President presented himself as the confident leader and the deeply caring human being he has always been known to be and will be. There were many great and uplifting moments as we watched our passing into a new era for our nation. Has there ever been a more powerfull dramatically realized rendition of our national anthem? Has poetry ever been constructed and artfully crafted with a beauty that captured the very soul of our country in these difficult but optimistic times? The masterpiece of words that was conceived and delivered by our country's first Youth Poet Laureate captured the nation with a rich understanding of who we are and who we need to become. As a person whose life has been centered in the arts, I was paralyzed by the power of this gifted young woman's art. And on that idea, what a profound deep breath of relief to see the arts re-incorporated into the fabric of our country again!

Amidst all the very fine moments the inauguration ceremony shared with the American people, there was one moment that defined the grandeur of the day for me.

Void of people, the vast acreage of that monumental area that connects the Lincoln Memorial to the George Washington Monument and onward to the steps of the mighty Capitol itself, were regiments of star-spangled banners - holding ground as symbols of those we lost due to the pandemic across our vast nation. They filled the grounds with majestic encompassment. The voice of all was spoken without words, or cheers or applause. There was the power of their silence, like snow, covering the ground. Evoking a gentle approval of the assembly on the Capitol steps, a unified light waving in the breeze spoke for those being remembered and those who could not be there - in fact, all who believe in The United States of America.

It was a dignified tribute to the Americans who were seated or standing at the facade of that great symbol of American strength, the Capitol, whose very halls and facade had been desecrated but a few weeks before. It was a formidable presence as the mild wind was giving life to the red, white and blue, as the seemingly endless flags quietly waved in the open free air of America.

And a quiet flapping hummed the strains of our national anthem throughout the proceedings.

The spirits of the dead and the living united in the blessing of a new administration. All was quiet. But there was one earthshaking moment that did not escape my observance. When the gracious Senator ended her opening address she affirmed that Democracy cannot be taken from us. And the television cameras from the station I was watching turned to the field of Old Glories. And like the miracle that *is* American Democracy there was suddenly a strong gust of wind across the landscape and *all* the banners unfurled in full for a brief moment in time and you could hear the loud flapping like an army of angels whose wings made a more joyful noise than hundreds of thousands of people clapping - the souls of the dead and the spirit of the living - united - in a cry to keep our fragile democracy alive.

The Mighty Oak

> ...
> *Silent, I turn to light*
> *Silent, I welcome birds*
> *Silent, I lift the children*
> *Silently reaching outward*
> *Silently holding tight*
> *And my roots go deep*
> *In this place I know*
> *Though I may be old*
> *Still I grow...*
> *For I was put here to make*
> *Something Beautiful*
> *Make something beautiful*
> *Before I go*
>
> SOMETHING BEAUTIFUL
> by Lynne Ahrens & Stephen Flaherty
> from the song cycle "Legacy"

There was a tree. It was a mighty oak. It stood tall on the corner of the avenue on which my childhood was spent. It towered atop the highest point on the steep slope of Homestead Avenue at the corner that adjoined it to the cross street named Monterey, which connected at a short distance to Woodbine Street on the other side. There it stood spreading its thick graceful branches over the avenue and the small cross street, uniting them in shade. It reached into the small wooded area that was a vacant lot and was home to many hours of play in my early childhood.

One would find that trees are very plentiful were a numerical census of living things be accounted. And each is special in its own right. But this tree held a majesty that set it apart and drew attention from many perspectives. Its height was gigantic in comparison to the other trees in the neighborhood - not quite a Sequoia but certainly a towering presence to the surrounding area. Its trunk was massive. Even the most broad shouldered of us children and those older could reach no more than halfway around the mighty stem that centered the layers of umbrella laced branches above. This was a powerful gift of nature.

Due to the behemoth-like girth of this stately oak, climbing it was a challenge of a higher order. It was reserved for only the most determined and fearless. Those who might be willing to accept the dare would need to also accept the brandishing of a punishment of scapes and bruises that were a certainty to be bestowed on the skin of any climber.

In addition to the prickly and densely-massed skin of the tree, the other sentry this mighty oak held in protecting its privacy was that the lowest set of branches were at a height of somewhere between twelve and fifteen feet from the ground. This was a monstrous feat for a young body to consider in taking on the challenge of possessing a view from the branches above.

An added consideration to be reckoned with in taking on the conquest of this neighborhood Mount Everest was the terrain of the ground surrounding the base of the tree. The mighty oak's roots made for hard, rutted, uneven ground in a wide circumference surrounding this local Hyperion. The stoic wooden plant also enjoyed the protective friendship of large in-ground pointed rocks and sizable boulders close enough to the main axis to complicate any reasonably safe dismount from the branches above.

Never would the adjective, *athletic*, even in the most exaggerated forgivenesses in poetic license, be applied to my nature as a child. Yes, I was a very fast runner. That was a skill I developed as a protective means to escape bullies and the aggressive gladiator-type kids in the neighborhood who were drawn to me by my diminutive size and muscle deprived physique.

I was always befriended when something required getting into a small space or to quickly retrieve a ball that had trespassed onto some private property where the cranky owner, who despised children and their play tactics, should come out to scold and threaten with empty claims of police incarceration. And I was the lightweight who would be called upon to rescue items caught in tree branches where the limbs were not strong enough to bear much weight or when standing on another's shoulders might suffice.

I had no fear of heights in those days. Today, please don't ask me to look down from anywhere higher than a first story apartment. Even then you have to make sure the vantage point is fully enclosed. I lost confidence in my dexterity in places of altitude where a keen sense of balance and security of courage are required after a near fatal accident hanging lighting instruments for a college theatrical production. I took a near header out of a drop ceiling only to be rescued by a fellow classmate who secured my legs until security obtained a large A-frame ladder to rescue me in what seemed like hours later. Since then my fear of heights is a bit harsh, especially when there is unobstructed space surrounding my location.

But in my childhood days and well into my early to mid-teens, no altitude could intimidate me. I especially loved climbing tall young trees, fifteen feet or higher, that grew in the several wooded areas near my home. I would climb as high as the mature saplings could bear my meager weight and I would ride the bending tops from one tree to the other as if I were Tarzan, a bird, or some kind of an orangutan.

If I did possess any real kind of athleticism in my childhood, this would have been my field of accomplishment. And since there were no competitive events or prize assessment procedures for tree swinging, my expertise went unrecognized and unrewarded. "If a child swings from tree to tree in the forest and there is no one there to see him, does…" Never mind.

Still there stood this mighty oak. Older boys in the neighborhood met the challenge and gained success in reaching the lower branches to claim their victory rights. I yearned to find my way to that place or beyond.

While not many knew of my Tarzan-like skills it was well known how much I loved to climb any tree that seemed to offer an invitation. It became fun sport with the older kids in the neighborhood to tease me about my inability to get into this behemoth of trees. There was always someone putting out the challenge to watch me try. There was a lot of humor found in watching me fail. Life is such that no one wants someone to be fully successful at things they do well. And my inability to conquer this tree gave cause to their false sense of superiority.

Not to outwit them or prove them wrong, but rather to satisfy my own desire and determination to rise up to those supple sturdy branches, my focus on accomplishing this only increased with my every failure to solve my problem. I *would* one day reach that height to survey my world from the view atop this grand creation of nature.

EXTOLLING THE ORDINARY

When my usual companions were otherwise engaged with family obligations or off pursuing their own special interests, I would make my way to the crest of the hill to the corner where the mighty oak spread its splendid branches. There I would calculate and devise my strategy of how I would get into that tree. If only I were a gecko with setae able to adhere to the tree via Van DerWaal's force or if I were a goat of Morocco's Argan Forest that can climb up to twenty five feet into a tree to feast on Argan fruit nuts. Alas, I was only a scrawny four and a half foot skinny kid of little physical strength.

It is a fact that numerous species of God's creatures can readily make their way to the zenith of their vertical travel routes. Size never seems to help or hinder them when the desire is there.

Those who made their way to the upper region of the tree seemed to gain an advantage from a running jump start to get them half way or more up the tree's trunk. Using the larger boulders as elevated launching points also proved a major aid to a few of the older guys.

Yet my small, light stature afforded no benefit for me in establishing sufficient thrust in such launchings.

I had a cousin who was two years older than me. He lived next door. Even though he was usually among the taunters and jeerers who teased and belittled me, he would secretly, when his own peers were not about, help me by letting me stand on his shoulders to try to gain some advantage in getting higher. I appreciated this even though there was something hypocritical in his not wanting others to see his kindness in caring about my efforts. I think he had a hidden desire to see me succeed at this - well, at anything.

My older brother suffered from serious asthmatic health challenges in his childhood years. Extensive exercise or activity was not safe for him. Because of this my parents extended an un-required over-protective aura in regards to myself as well. Safety and caution were enforced on me as much as possible.

My cousin once spied on me and followed me on one of my solo sojourns into the nearby woods to see what I was up to and likely with intentions of trying to scare me. Instead he witnessed my arboreal escape into the heights of the young trees.

I didn't personally get to see his being astounded as he witnessed my aerial feats but it would be safe to say he was flabbergasted at my dexterity and lack of fear.

He decided not to attempt to scare me but instead identified his presence and asked me how I did it and why I wasn't afraid. He could have called me Junior Tarzan but I had to settle for "Monkey-boy."

Whatever was behind his offerings to help me conquer the oak, I appreciated his help. Several years later he spent a great deal of time teaching me to play basketball which was a farfetched dream of mine given my Lilliputian stature. But he took the time anyway and taught me the basic skills and rules of the game. And his help in lifting me higher up the trunk of the tree afforded me knowledge of the terrain I would need to know for the journey up that I would eventually have to make on my own.

I suspect my cousin was eager to see me relax into the more defiant and daredevil side of my guarded nature. For a while we would ride bikes together on escapades beyond the parameters of where our parents allowed us to travel. Those days ended too quickly once he made the basketball team at our grade school and later went on to high school a year ahead of me.

Scansorial climbing (climbing by clawed creatures) which is used by raccoons, porcupines and squirrels shows that larger animals are challenged by the prospect of their falling. Scientifically, smaller bodied creatures exercise a more acrobatic technique in climbing that allows them to scurry quicker by using a maximum velocity that allows a greater surface area to volume ratio, which reduces the likelihood of falling.

Had my juvenile mind known of this scientific understanding at the time, I would have fretted less about my diminutive stature in conquering the height. My smallness and my lightness were my strength. I just didn't know. And one day, on my own, putting aside the reality that I would be scratched and cut by the thick bark on the tree, I catapulted myself up the tree to the extended branches which reached out above me. My lack of weight put little pressure on the thick bark and the speed of my movement allowed me to hang on and hold sturdy clumps of bark whenever I dislodged weaker coverings as I rose upward. I made it! I climbed the mighty oak! And I did it on my own natural ability.

I didn't see my cousin until the next day. And when I did I told him of my triumph. He made me show him. Once I was in the branched elevation, he joined me and we watched the occasional cars go by from our aerial vantage. Once there, it seemed like the sky was the limit and so I climbed higher, something he preferred not to do. Because of the thickness of the branches, the spacing between the rising limbs was lengthy and while I was not frightened to go higher; I was sensible enough to not over-extend my ability to safely shimmy up to reach beyond my body length.

I was governed by knowing I needed an assured footing when I decided to come down. The last thing I needed to spoil my crowning achievement was a Fire Department rescue to tarnish my glory.

I did rise high enough to look over the rooftops of all the houses that lined the hill to the bottom, where I could view the playground that filled the block at the base of the slope that defined the street where I lived.

None of the adults in the neighborhood condoned their kids climbing that tree. It was considered dangerous. And as parents usually find what their kids have been up to through some guarded secret communication network, mine learned of my success in defeating the challenge of the mighty oak. My reward from them was the promise of severe punishment if they learned of my ever climbing that tree again. And so I resigned to obey my parents and never climb up to my new found heaven again.

My father was especially curious as to how I got down after my climbs as the drop to the ground was considerably lengthy from the height of those first branches. I explained that I just lowered myself holding onto the sturdy branch out away from the rocks and roots below and let myself drop. My small size lessened the force of gravity on my impact when I landed on the ground.

My conquering of the Mount Everest of trees took place during the late Spring. And the summer passed and this little "monkey-man" never broke his promise to his parents to never risk the danger of going up again. But later that year, in the mid-Fall, l I broke that promise and went up into the tree again.

It was late October and several friends and I were out "ringing doorbells," an exercise of Mischief Night, part of the Halloween festivities that we executed as a self-exonerated passage considered righteously part of being a kid. Pretty much all we would do is ring a household's doorbell then run and hide behind a nearby bush or some other location of refuge. One of my friends had an older brother who had given him a homemade device that he was just itching to make use of.

It was a wooden spool, a remnant of sewing thread, nailed to a one by three board, only a few feet in length. There were a few feet of Venetian blind cord wrapped around the spool. When you placed the device against a large window or an aluminum storm door and pulled the cord, it vibrated with a noise slightly reminiscent of rapid gunfire.

There was a home across the street from the Mighty Oak that was adjacent to the corner of the wooded lot where the grand tree stood. The house had both a large picture window and an aluminum storm door. Despite the seemingly obvious perfection of the house as a target for my friend's device, I thought it not a wise choice for him to test his demonic toy for the first time on that particular house. I knew the home belonged to a local policeman. And while his squad car was not parked in the driveway or out front, it seemed a foolish target. I was labeled a scaredy-cat. The logic of the others was that the house was just across the street from the wooded lot where there were ample hiding places amidst large rocks, undergrowth and the trees. The officer likely was not home and only his wife would be there to frighten or startle.

My pal, overzealous with his prankster toy, crept across the front yard into the shrubbery under the picture window, poised to take the poor unsuspecting woman inside off her guard. We all were ready to run and hide in the small wooded lot.

When our anxious friend pulled the cord and buzzed the window and took flight, her husband in the squad car was coming up the street and then pulled in in-front of the property. The woman had come outside to see what caused the vibration on her window and in hopes of catching sight of the culprit who did this. The gang scattered into the wooded lot. Some ran all the way through and out the back side scampering across the yard of the home that sat on the other side. My pal with his buzz-stick, or whatever it might be called, ran into the smaller wooded lot right next to the officer's home. It led into a deeper wooded area that went for miles behind those homes.

Scared to death of being caught and blamed as the sole perpetrator, I like the true scaredy-cat I was, used my feline agility to scamper up into the branches of the Mighty Oak. Below, the officer searched the wooded location in hopes of catching mischievous Halloween revelers with his powerful flashlight. It was dark and so I could not see where any of my friends were hiding or where they had gone. He likely caught unidentifiable sight of a few of my friends as they ran off in all directions. He was only intending to return the scare imposed on his wife. He never once pointed his light up into the tree where I was cowering. After a few moments inside his home, the officer returned to his car and drove off. I wasn't sure if he would make a few passes around the block in hopes of catching my friends or other revelers he could keep in line. So I sat for a while in the elevated darkness of my arboreal sanctuary.

Time passed slower than I had ever felt before. Then I heard my father calling me home. It was curfew time. I desperately started planning my descent from the tree hoping my father's continuing calls for me would not place me at the reason for the recent commotion. Even worse was the punishment I knew would be waiting for not responding to my father's call.

It seemed like an eternity was passing. Eventually I deemed it safe to drop from the tree. It didn't seem the officer would be doubling back.

Of course I had never climbed the tree in the dark before. There was a streetlight at the corner that was out. It was part of of my friends' reasoning that it would make hiding easier when targeting the home with the device. Dropping from the tree required knowing where the ground was clear of rocks and the immense roots that made for the rough terrain at the base of the tree. Because of the darkness, I could not clearly see the ground area below. I chanced it, guessed, and dropped myself down.

Bad guess! I landed one foot half on a large root and the other on a large stone. It was a far cry from a safe landing. I severely twisted both of my ankles on impact.

They were throbbing with pain. I hobbled down the hill noting well that gravity was still not being my friend because my downward motion on the incline of the hill seemed to force me to put extra weight on my ankles as I did my best to keep upright and balanced.

Once home I told the whole truth of the evening's escapades and as I fully expected, my parents were neither amused or pleased by my lack of judgment in partaking in such a prank. I was sent immediately to bed and there was no sympathy, empathy or any "… thy" for my sore ankles. More upset at being punished than hurting, I never even thought to see that both my ankles were swelling up.

In the morning I could barely stand let alone walk. My father had already left for work and my mother wasn't in the mood for rehashing anything about my behavior of the night before. She took the stance that if I thought I was grown up enough to behave in the way I had, I was also grown up enough to walk off the pain I was feeling. She hoped I would learn my lesson by working through the pain. I was walking so there clearly was nothing broken.

Fortunately, my aunt from next door was driving us kids to school that morning so I didn't have to walk. The school was a slightly longer than one exact mile away.

I know it is a familiar thing of great amusement for folks to hear from people who tell tales of walking to school in snow and rain and cold weather, but I truly did have to walk to school almost every morning for that slightly lengthened mile. And at lunchtime, which was only an hour long, I had to walk home, eat and return to school. And yes, many times it was often through rain, snow, sleet or cold weather. And at times extremely high temperatures in the spring.

By the time morning recess came I could not stand and I was helped to the school nurse who determined I had two sprained ankles. When I semi-confessed to her how it happened - I only told her I jumped from a considerable height from a tree - no need to confess to the borderline criminal activity - she felt confident in her assessment of my bodily damage. My father had to be called out of work to pick me up and take me home.

I had to stay off my feet for a few days and missed school. My father likely was docked pay for having to leave to get me. He and my mom both worked hard to give my brother and I the things we needed and often things that we just wanted. My little prank produced more guilt on my part about his lost wages than the general disappointment I gave my parents.

I recovered within a few days and took an exploratory stroll up to the corner of the Mighty Oak to survey exactly what I landed on.

I never went up into that tree again. I found contentment sitting on the large boulder at its base and soaking in its shade whenever we played ball on the short cross street that began at that corner. I will always treasure the view I had of the neighborhood the time I dared to go as high as I could. And I never thought lightly of the beauty and majesty of its strength and presence hanging over the corner where many memorable moments of my childhood were spent. Whenever I hear the Joyce Kilmer poem, I envision that tree.

After I graduated from college, my parents moved from that neighborhood. I often would drive myself around the few blocks that held the history of my childhood. And I would always be sure to check to see if my friend, the Mighty Oak, the one that saved me from a trip to the police station, the one that taught me to believe in my own abilities, the one that watched over my growing from child to young man, was still there. It remained the landmark that continually reminded me that all is right with the world.

I hadn't made one of my random returns to check on the old neighborhood in a few years. My brief sojourns to my childhood reveries diminished once I took up permanent residence in the concrete alleyways of New York City. But recently I had the chance and was afforded the opportunity to peruse the old neighborhood. I saw my childhood home. It had changed physically in color and the landscaping around it was new. The hill I climbed so many times with ease with my friends, often to get to the top to sled its ample length in the winter snowstorms more than a half century ago, seemed steeper. Somehow that made it grander in my recollections of the days and years spent. When I got to the apex of the incline, the place where Homestead corner-connects to Monterey, there was a ghostly emptiness in my memory.

The oak was gone. The wooded lot had been cleared decades ago to build a large ranch style home. At that time the great oak tree had been spared. I imagine several owners have inhabited that home. But the latest owners seemed to have made a decision to chop down that bastion of my childhood and memories. Maybe its immense size became a threat to the structure of their home. Maybe it was struck by lightning in a summer thunderstorm and was severely damaged and needed to come down. I know it stood on that corner for well over a hundred years. Maybe it was just time to go.

In life, we stumble upon our friends as we make our journey. We do not necessarily choose them. And we never own our friends. They are loaned to us. And we do not get to keep them forever. But we hold onto them as long as we can. Like an undersized child determined to wrap his too short arms around a gigantic oak to embrace the life of that tree to experience its majesty to the fullest measure, we hold on. We hold on for dear life. That tree was my friend. It was as important to me as the kids I played with and the neighbors who helped me grow. From up in its far reaching arms I saw the expanse of my world and learned to embrace it. I have lost connection with most of the kids I grew up with. As time has passed, the neighbors and parents of my friends have quietly exited this world to leave me with a richness of a wonderful childhood remembered. I have mourned each of their passings. My last trip to the old neighborhood gave me one more deep sense of loss - The Mighty Oak.

I will always go back and try to absorb the spirit of that time and remember the people, the events and now... the tree that gave it life.

Angels, Shrinks & Revelations

When I was younger, so much younger than today
I never needed anybody's help in any way
But now those days are gone, I'm not so self assured
Now I find I changed my mind
I've opened up the doors

HELP
Words & music by
John Lennon & Paul McCartney

We all have our own truths. For the most part, we are not in any way exactly like our counterparts that we share our space with in our limited square footage upon this planet. People never see things in the same perceived manner as others within their own circles of fellow humans. Experience can define how we understand it. A healthy perception of whatever event penetrates our senses and perceptions mostly align with the shared ideas of those we choose to share our sociological exchanges with. From this we establish a kind of commonality that we haphazardly define as truth.

As our daily lives wind and ramble through the moments of our existence, we accustom ourselves to an unconscious compromise concerning just about everything we experience. This, I surmise, is what most, or at least some, people would define as normal. I do not believe in "normal." I much prefer to champion uniqueness. I find this makes my life richer. And, if I am being totally honest, it can also leave me stranded and confused in a spider-web-like-maze of my own making.

Most times, because I alone have charted the mental labyrinth on my own, I am able to find my way back to the world in which I enjoy compromising and sharing like perceptions with those I deem my friends and associates. Via individuals or a general public - I can assure my sometimes self-questioning psyche that I am functioning as a sane and well balanced individual.

I suppose the question does remain - "Just because I think I am psychologically sound, does that make it the truth?" After all, doesn't that require a collective belief in the notion that there is an existing reality that goes by the concept called "normal"?

Before I construct one of my labyrinths and frame it in one of my usual hall of funhouse mirrors, let me explain, no, let me admit, there have been times I have buried myself in a primeval chaos of my own making, where I found myself desperately calling from that bottomless pit for some kind of help. It becomes evident that my own "true" isn't always the answer to sustain my balance on the tightrope of sanity in the world at large.

Conceitedly, I will state that there have been less than a handful of times that I have yelled for a proverbial life preserver to be thrown from the deck of conformity so I can be rescued from the raging ocean of my own confusion. And when these moments have come into my life, I have done what most conforming, normal people do. I found a psychiatrist to direct me on a healthy journey.

Fortunately, amidst my individualized, unconventional ideologies, there has always been the comfort of knowing that there is no shame in needing, or acknowledging the need for, help and guidance from professionals skilled in the art of unraveling people from poisonous or troubling thoughts that obstruct calm and from what may be keeping someone from a healthy life journey. I have never felt there was an element of shame in needing this assistance. Maybe that is due to my attitude that shame doesn't figure into my feelings about much of anything. But it is far more likely that because I have known so many people who regularly visit their therapist I viewed it as something chic or trendy.

Maturity is a lifelong process. Engaging a doctor or social worker to help you put your life on course, or keep it there, or at least within your control, is neither chic nor trendy. I know that now. But I didn't know it when I connected with my first psychiatric doctor.

In my early thirties I decided to venture out on my own after seven years of working in the field of talent representation. I started my own company managing talented actors with whom I had developed a relationship during my time with two different agencies. And there were actors outside of that scope I also chose to represent in aiding their career goals. I left the talent agency that I had been employed by for almost four years. And I was fortunate that several of the folks I worked with sought me out after I ventured out on my own.

My wife of that time and I had a spacious apartment in the Audubon Circle section of Washington Heights in upper Manhattan. We had several extra rooms which served no function in our daily living there. It was economically sound to use one of these rooms as an office for my new business. The one chosen had a separate entrance which would make it ideal as an office and provide privacy for meetings solely for business purposes. The apartment had doubled as a doctor's office and residence before we moved in. Meetings were not likely as the heart of the industry was more than a hundred blocks south in the Times Square area. In the nineteen eighties, it was neither fashionable nor considered totally safe by the predominantly white folks who orbited within my circles to live that far north on the island of Manhattan. Moving about above ninety sixth street, except for the Columbia University area, was not welcomed by the (again) predominantly white society that filled positions in the entertainment industry. People were just unaware that the Audubon Circle section of the Heights was as gentrified, if not more so, than the more fashionable neighborhoods of the Upper West Side. The area sported beautiful architecturally designed apartment buildings, museums, a fabulous old cemetery that held gravesites of many famous and historical people, and had magnificent views of the Hudson River. But people weren't versed in going that far north on the island to visit or do business.

Choosing to work from my home base created an extended isolation for me. I no longer was making daily trips to mid-town and I was no longer part of an environment that provided easy socialization for making new friends and contacts. I hadn't thought about that when I made the decision.

It didn't take long for signs of aggravated discomfort to take hold on me.

It was not so intense as to threaten my sanity, but for the first time in my life, I began to think that having a "shrink" to talk to would calm the uneasy feelings and self- conversations I was beginning to have. With the help of a trusted friend I contacted an organization that provided health services for professionals who would only charge rates that were commensurate with a person's income. Just starting out on my own, my income was limited. I would learn years later that health service is no different than any other business - you get what you pay for.

I had several telephone interviews with a number of doctors. Through my explorations I decided I would best be served by a female doctor. I think I always felt that women were more attuned to sensitivities of human frailties than men - a myth I likely learned in early life stemming from conformity and aspiring to normality. I felt there would be no judgment of my vulnerability as a male. I chose a woman to take my issues to.

At my first appointment she came across far less amiable than she had in our telephone conversations. To put it succinctly she was quite austere. I deduced this was nothing more than a veneer of her professionalism. It was difficult to get any sense of her as a person because her office/session room was kept very dark. It was very dimly lit by only two sources. There was a small table lamp that I would guess was illuminated by at best, a forty-watt lightbulb. Perhaps it was controlled on a dimmer from her desk. The lampshade too was dark. It was a deep rich wine color. I am a huge proponent of low level lighting. One of my dearest of friends once commented upon visiting our home, "Can we get some light in here? What are you, the Prince of Darkness?" For my dear friend I agreed to brighten the room but *my* eye comfort got dimmer.

I was comforted by the sufficient glow of the yellow light that lit the area around the squared off oversized stuffed chair where I was seated. It provided a veil of comfort as I settled into this new experience.

The other source of illumination came from a large chrome plated silver orb with an open bottom that floated over the doctor, supported by an elongated tube that curved through the air from a distant corner. I could not see the actual ground point or clearly determine that the tube was as equally shiny as the structure of the sphere which it supported. It hung in the air over her head like some distant planet. When my short number of visits with this doctor ended, I would more aptly describe it as a personalized Death Star, from the Star Wars films.

At the time the fixture was most impressive and I imagine quite expensive. The brightness, or lack thereof, was definitely controlled by a dimmer on her desk. At one point, she increased the luminosity enough for her to find her misplaced pen on her desk but not enough to disturb the ambience she meticulously constructed for our sessions. And she never sat fully in her spotlight, giving a less than clear vision of herself. I thought of the great and powerful Oz. But even he showed more of himself.

She asked me why I felt I needed to be there and I confided the unrest I was feeling about isolation and some troubling questions I was having about working alone in the new business I had started. She took notes. She asked me about my marriage which at the time was well intact. She asked me about my parents and what I was like as a child. All the questions she asked seemed familiar from movies and television shows I had seen. The last question of that session was about my religious upbringing. I told her I was raised Catholic but it had been well over ten years since I considered myself Catholic. I was a self-practicing Christian of no assigned denomination. I confessed I did not like any organized religions. She thanked me and told me we would continue our conversation at the next session. As I exited, she never got up or acknowledged my departure; she sat head down scribbling some notes on the pad on her faintly glowing desk.

Our second meeting she initiated with her observations from our first meeting. She seemed more occupied with ideas that I might have trepidations about growing into being my own boss with my business. It surprised me because I made it clear what I wanted help with was my fear of isolation. But she was the doctor and I had put my trust in her care. I explained that I was doing the same work I had performed for the previous seven years and that I was confident in my ability to perform well. And I edged toward asking if we could talk about my main objective in being there. She bristled slightly and said I had to trust her, that there were no simple understandings and the more she knew about me the quicker we would get to the heart of the matter. She asked me about my parents' religious practices. I told her my father was a very devout Catholic and that he was active in church groups and activities and even played golf with one of the priests on occasion. I said my mom was also a member of a few church groups but that she wasn't likely as hard-line a Catholic as my dad, as her father was a Protestant and her mother a Catholic. I told her I doubted my mother was as committed to the strictness of Catholic doctrine as my dad but that they both were solid practicing devout Catholics. I confessed I feared that I somehow concerned them with my Catholic-on-Christmas only practice. The doctor almost smiled.

When the session came to an end, she said I should really think through if I really wanted to run my own business because her experiences informed her that Christians do not make good businessmen. And we would talk further next session.

I was much taken aback by the rather blunt and professionally questionable statement with which she left me. And as I thought about what she implied I also thought about her name. While I never asked or cared about her religious ties, I deduced from her name that she likely practiced or at one time practiced some form of the Jewish faith. And I wondered what antisemitism in reverse might be called.

EXTOLLING THE ORDINARY

The next session was a bit strained. I felt a little defensive and unwilling to be fully open with her. She probed about my family and my relationship with them and then started making assumptions and implying that I held deep resentments against my parents. Nothing could ever be further from the truth or reality. My parents devoted their lives to my brother and myself in helping us in every way they could.

I told her so and she responded that my defensiveness was a good sign that we were making breakthroughs. And she asked me about my brother. "You haven't really said much about him. Tell me about him."

I explained that we were very different in most ways. Almost antithetical. And I confessed that because of that we were not all that close at that time.

"Tell me about his family. Is he married? Where does he live?" She interrogated.

"He lives down South with his life partner. They have a beautiful home where…" I was cut off.

"Life partner?" Her

"Yes" Me

"Is he gay?!?" Her

"Yes." Me

"Well that explains everything," she blurted out, "you are resisting your own homosexuality."

"That is total nonsense," I told her

"Homosexuality is hereditary. If your brother is then you are as well. This is what you are fighting." She gloated like she just won the Pulitzer.

I told her she was misinformed. Firstly, about me. Secondly about her unfounded and unprofessional assumptions about homosexuality. And I realized that maybe my problems were not so bad or deep. This woman attacked my religious upbringing, took some unfounded Freudian stance that I held ill feelings toward my parents, and was now making unscientific and effrontery statements about my sexuality. I wasn't looking for a quick fix when I entrusted myself to this woman's care. But apparently "quick fix" was her methodology. I did not come for that and I didn't feel that even though I was only paying fifty dollars a session I would settle for therapy from Lucy of the *Peanuts* comic strip. I assembled my thoughts and told her, as I had intended to do at the end of this session, I was taking a business trip to Los Angeles for the next few weeks and I would let her know when I got back. This was the absolute truth except now I had no intention of contacting her when I returned.

She erupted like a volcano spewing out that I was avoiding facing my issues. I did my best to withhold my temper and need to lash back as she continued what I considered unprofessional and uncalled-for behavior. When she ran out of steam I told her I would not be back. I resented her unprofessional statements about my religion, her sophomoric Psych 101 calculations about by relationship with my parents and most of all her ignorant understanding of homosexuality. She became genuinely angry now - opposed to the self congratulating passion motivating her previous behavior. She accidentally nudged the dimmer controlling the Death Star and the lights came up full as she rose from behind her desk like the Kraken called from the ocean depths, she scrambled to gain control of her lighting. This was the first time I ever completely saw her. She was an immensely obese woman and she may as well have been stripped naked in a public place because her embarrassment in revealing her identity/size was profound. She spurted hateful anti-gay phrases at me. I stood in disbelief but told her with confidence that I thought she was unfit to practice in her field because she was whatever the reverse of antisemitism is, and a fraud and a quack and her homophobic issues should disqualify her from having a license. And I must confess that somewhere in my rage I made a disparaging comment on her obesity.

I watched the Kraken sink back into her depths under her glaring spotlight as I exited her office. Outside I felt sorry for her. I felt sorrier for the patients she had a hold on or would attract in the future. And I somehow felt free of the issues I had thought were bothering me. I also swore to myself that even though this had been a bad choice on my part, and not a fair example of psychiatric practice, I would never put my faith in a shrink again. What were my angels thinking to let me subject myself to this?

Swearing to oneself is a bit of a hollow gesture. Who is betrayed if you break your promise? Only yourself. Time healed my wound and left no visible scar. Only I could still feel the impression it dented on my brain.

When the marriage that was well intact during my visits with Dr. Death Star began showing surface cracks, I was eager to get my wife to talk to someone professionally to help her with unanswered questions she was wrestling with after her mother suddenly passed away at a much too young age. Her mother was her best friend, well, certainly her closest friend. It was hard for her mother to relinquish her oldest daughter to marriage when we decided to wed. She struggled to lose that resentment but in time succeeded. But I felt my wife was harboring hostilities toward me for being a cause for her to have moved away, distancing her from her mom. Losing her mother was a deeply painful experience and because her mother died so young there were volumes of thoughts that weren't finding a place in her otherwise understanding and usual sense of keen reasoning.

My wife, unlike myself, was a religious soul. She deepened her faith after seeing the Franco Zefferelli film about Saint Francis of Assisi and as odd as it seems her trust and belief in God intensified after that experience. When her mom was taken from her she did not know how to process her anger and grievance against the God who she still felt a need to trust but felt had disappointed her. With her mother gone and her God seemingly having abandoned her she focused much of her resentment and confusion in my direction. In fairness some of that was likely directed my way because of my lack of attention to needs she held me responsible for as well. But I wanted her to get help in getting past the unsettled feelings she was facing more and more each day.

It took a long time, months, maybe more than a year, for me to convince her to find a professional to talk to. Eventually she did. She too chose a female practitioner.

She trusted her and the doctor opened other issues that in time helped her reason things out. She liked this doctor and trusted her. And she felt the sessions and the continued therapy were helping her. The doctor was a feminist. She only took female patients. And while she seemed helpful to my wife, I quietly held that she was a bit of a misandrist. Not that I shouldn't own responsibility for some of my wife's problems but more and more *all* that was wrong slowly became my fault only. Not completely. My wife's father and the machismo of Italian-American culture were standing beside me.

I think my wife felt concerned that everything was becoming my fault and responsibility. The therapist suggest we live apart for a while and I conceded. I think in a session my wife said I wasn't all that bad or something like that which made Mme. Therapist curious to actually meet me. An invitation was extended for me to join a session. It was an invitation that I surmise was made with an intent of proving my masculine reticence to truly help and confront the issues at hand. I truly believe Madame was disappointed when I accepted.

Her office was her apartment. It was one of those wonderful old apartments on the Upper West Side of Manhattan. I arrived with my wife, exactly on time.

When we entered she told us to sit within the squared-off sofa arrangement that filled the center of her living room office. I sat on the long sofa with my back to the entrance door. My wife sat on the small loveseat that was cornered to my right. The therapist asked if I was allergic to animals and I said no. Truth was I sometimes had small reactions to certain breeds of cats. She had a dog - a German Shepherd - and a Siamese cat. She stated that her pets were not aggressive but they did not take warmly to strangers. I told her I knew to not approach animals but to let them come to you if they so desired. She told me the session was not about me. And that her animals would just stay away. I nodded understanding.

As the session got underway with her asking questions that implied that I somehow dominated my wife's every move and decision throughout our almost fourteen years of marriage, I quietly answered simply and directly without any sense of being defensive. I pretty much guessed her intentions and approach long before I sat on her well worn couch. Her intent was to rile me.

As we sat conversing I felt two small furry legs make their way down my left side from my neck. Then the second set down from the right side. The Siamese had wrapped itself around my neck from the back side of the sofa and was nuzzling the left side of my head and gleefully purring.

The therapist became mildly distracted and asked me if I would like to have her remove the cat. I said, "No, I am fine. She is very loving. She is a she isn't she?" To which the doctor affirmed and recomposed herself. Of course the cat was female. No doubt the dog was as well. And a new line of questioning began. A few minutes later her German Shepard came up on the couch and planted its head in my lap. I began petting her as she nuzzled closer to me warming to my attention.

The questioning halted as the therapist sat watching, more than mildly confounded by the situation. "I don't understand this. They never behave this way. This is most distracting. Perhaps we should end this part of the session and you should leave Kevin so your wife and I may continue."

"Certainly. Sure." I said inquiring if there was a preferred way to untangle myself from the animals without startling them or upsetting them.

She told me I could just get up and they would be fine. I did. And they were. But she wasn't. I retrieved my coat and left. The angels that were looking out for me might have been more instructive to have me look heavenward to thank my wife's beloved Saint Francis for coming to my defense. I am sure my wife was counting on him to look out for her. But he brought the animals to my defense, affirming my belief that spiritual entities don't take sides. No matter what was or would be said about me in that session or ones to come, I rested assured that my character and dignity could never be truly libeled or maligned again in that room…at least by the doctor.

And as I walked through the Upper West Side making my way to the uptown number One train, the sun shone and I smiled even more brightly. Once again I had survived this thing called therapy without having to don a straitjacket.

I may have survived the vengeance of her therapist and the challenge of that moment, but my marriage was not destined to the same fate. It took another thirteen years but the slings and arrows of outrageous mis-fortune caught up with us and the structure of life as I had known and wanted it finally crashed.

I had made no promises over the years of staying away from those who practiced psychological healing. The days of the Death Star Doctor were far behind me. And wasn't I the victorious one when the shrink who never really knew me sought to assign me blame for the early cracks in the marriage that now had seemingly run its course. This time was different though. We had a child.

My deep emotional unrest outweighed my negative experiences in dealing with professionals in the psychiatric field. I knew they couldn't all be bad. I knew some were quite good and obviously there are ones who are astounding who manage to keep people returning to their lairs for years and years on end. This was not my case to date. But I was ready to give it another go.

A friend recommended a guy who he had met with for one session or so but decided that he did not need or perhaps just did not want to plunge into the process. He chose to regulate his problems on his own. But he recommended this guy. He also told me that he was a little on the expensive side. I checked with my insurance and they were only willing to pay roughly one third of this guy's fee. I felt I had learned my lesson in trusting people who operated on the cheap side and figured I would pretend I could afford this man's insights and I took the plunge.

This was already a different kind of experience. I did not have to endure the hassles of the subway and the noise and distractions of New York City streets and pedestrian traffic. All I had to do was drive myself there in the quiet and serenity of my car.

The office was about seventy-five miles from my home. But it was only half that distance to get there if I went from my place of work. And the long ride home would give me time to reflect and/or clear my head from the experience. It was worth the try. The doctor's office was an annex to his home. It was located in a lovely coastal town in Connecticut. It might have been more enticing if the locale was on the waterfront but alas, you cannot have everything. His home was a few miles inland and it took me a while to find it as I slowly meandered along small back roads. I developed a sense that because of the sequestered location alone, I could trust that my secrets and sensitivities were safe in that they would never be shared, this place being so far off the beaten path of the masses. His place was atop a long climbing hill.

I slowly made my way along the narrow roadway which I could not tell whether it was actually a road or if it was his private driveway. A short way along there was what appeared to be a small town dump. This might have been disconcerting had my usual sick sense of humor not kicked in. I thought to myself, "Well, they won't have far to go if they decide my case is hopeless and have to dump my body."

When I approached the crest of the hill I could see what I gathered was the doctor's office. It was then that I realized it must also be his home. There was a small squared off area marked for the patients. It was nearest to the entrance marked for his office.

This place was cute. Really, "cute" is the most precise way to describe it. It was cottage-like and there were colorful flowers planted around the front and sides of the structure. And maybe it was my desperation that this be a different kind of experience than my previous encounters with therapists, or maybe I was so nervous that it had an hallucinatory effect on me, but the setting seemed like a location in a Hans Christian Anderson fairy tale. While it was comforting it was equally as disconcerting to my cynical presupposition that I was about to subject myself to an avoidable harrowing experience.

With trepidation I opened the door into the tiniest waiting room I had ever encountered. At best, the space was five feet by five feet. There was a simple wooden bench along the wall adjacent to the door that

I assumed was the office entrance. There was a tasteful simple sign on the door asking folks not to knock, that the doctor would allow you in for your appointment. There was something very civilized about this despite the seemingly regimented rule.

Fortunately there was someone else in the waiting area - a mother waiting for her teenage son. She told me her son should be out any minute, that the doctor was very precise with his schedule. She said it in a friendly manner that somehow neutralized what under other circumstances would have mildly agitated my aversion about regimentation. My inclination to defiance of such things was a hangover from the late sixties and seventies where "Keep Off The Grass" signs posed a threat to democracy in my generation. And yes, there was a "Keep Off The Grass" sign on the small area of lawn at the front of the cottage. Other than her kindness in pacing my waiting time, the woman said nothing.

I was early. I knew that. So waiting was not a problem. I felt that somehow I would know it was safe to go in if the young man came out with a smile on his face. That was the case. The doctor walked him to the door and I got a brief look at him before he shut the door saying he would be "right with" me, which he was.

I was let into the room, the office, and he closed the door behind me. It was a warm and spacious room. It had the feel of a closed-in porch or atrium but at the same time felt like an old English library or study. If the cottage gave the impression of a fairy tale setting, this office equally called to mind a perfect choice for a psychiatrist's study or at least an ingenious set for Professor Higgins in *Pygmalion*.

The doctor himself looked like he was sent to this locale by Central Casting. He kind of looked like Freud but there was something detachedly welcoming in his demeanor. If he were smoking a pipe it would have been too too perfect to be believable. He wasn't. But I saw one on his desk several sessions later, although he never smoked or touched it during our sessions.

He had a deep and quiet voice. It was soothing but not hypnotic. I quickly leaned toward trusting him. The win-over could draw a parallel to a small child losing all fear when poised to sit on the lap of a strange man in a red and white suit at the special Christmas display in the local department store or mall.

He asked me about myself, never attempting to direct a topic within my life story. He asked me who had recommended him and seemed surprised when I told him. Something in his eyes, in his face registered a guarded astonishment, like he may have felt he left an unfavorable impression on my friend. Then in a flash of a moment he digested the information with a mild relishing and returned to his stoic demeanor.

He wrote occasionally on his fresh steno pad. For fifty minutes he listened and occasionally presented me with a question to keep the monologue I was giving flowing. Ten minutes before the end of the session he spoke.

There was a genuinely quiet smile as he told me he felt he could help guide me to a comfortable place about my divorce. He said, "It is possible you really do not need my help at all. You feel you need help. So as long as you feel that, we can explore what you need to know about yourself to deal with this disappointment. You seem like a nice sincere person. But being nice is not addressing what you are really feeling. ... We will see what you decide. I will see you next week at the same time."

He walked me to the door. And he opened it. I turned to thank him and as I walked out I ran into the door. Not the one he opened. The one attached to the other side of the door frame. I opened it and turned back and said. "Therapy. It's about opening doors. I get it!" He gave me a wary smile, more like a smirk, and said, "You won't be able to hide behind that sense of humor of yours with me." He gave me a Santa Claus wink, not an assuring or flirtatious one but one that definitively showed he meant business and I should be prepared for that. He definitely knew who was naughty or nice.

I closed the second door as I exited and I heard the door of the inner sanctum close as well.

"Who is this guy!!!! I really like him." I walked to my car feeling like I had somehow already been partially helped. As I looked back at the cottage I think I was actually wondering if some kind of magic had just transpired. I started my car and began the 75 mile journey to what was now my broken home.

During my weeks of visits to the cottage on the hill I told the doctor of all the complexities feeding into the pending divorce. (No I will not publish them here.) My soon to be ex and I were meeting with a lawyer/counselor team to handle our divorce. It was her choice and I insisted she cover the financial costs because being released from our vows was what she needed to follow her intentions.

I liked the team. I said very little during our meetings/sessions. I was confident they would look at the situation and grant me what it was that *I* wanted from the settlement - joint-equal custody of our daughter. My sessions with the movie image perfect doctor in the cottage on the hill helped me hold a confidence I likely did not have about things before our sessions.

I don't know why I was able to feel this way because in truth, the good doctor never really said much of anything to me. That was until several weeks into our sessions he asked if he could make an observation. My immediate thought was a combination of "It's about time, what have I been paying for?" and anticipated joy that I might grasp some tool to help me feel better about myself and my sad situation.

He looked at me with a more serious look than his usual mysterious seriousness. "I think one of the key issues that is preventing you from dealing honestly and openly with your situation is you are owning a serious level of Catholic guilt."

I stared at him with an intense disbelief of what I had just heard. Was this man just another version of the mean obese woman under her glowing orb, wanting to slap some clichés from a textbook on me? Was he belittling by character and proud individualism by reducing me to some relic from my past I never chose to own? My head was rushing and swirling in so many forms of effrontery and disbelief I couldn't keep up with the tornado of hurt, fear, disappointment and the audacity of being lied to that I couldn't separate one thought or feeling from the other. All these weeks of quiet trust were suddenly a storm front of immense discomfort.

"Fuck you!" I said. "I haven't allowed myself to be governed or controlled by my Catholic upbringing since I was seventeen years old. This is horse-shit!" And I spewed story after story of events and things I knew about Catholicism that angered me and caused me to shut out any desire to align with that or any formalized institution ever again.

EXTOLLING THE ORDINARY

When I finished my tirade, he stopped and looked at me. I couldn't tell if he was angry with my outburst or if he was stunned by my foul language, which I had never used before with him, or if he was just calming me down with his own centered presence.

After a brief period of complete silence he quietly said, "I am going to read to you a number of things you have said over this past many weeks." He lifted his steno pad and began reading statement after statement, flipping through the many pages of this spiral bound document of our weeks together. When he was finished, or more accurately, when he sensed I got the complete picture, he set the pad down and looked at me with one of his wizardly smiles full of honest wisdom and assurance and the kindness his starched demeanor tried so hard to disguise.

We sat quietly and eventually he said, "If that isn't Catholic guilt, what is it?"

I'm not sure I ever looked that deeply into myself as I did at that moment. And in a quite voice, I dropped my head in what was either shame or honest resignation and said, "Catholic guilt."

He told me to think about what this meant and that we would discuss it further and unravel this thing from the person I thought I was and wanted to be. On my ride home I began to feel released from a number of frustrations about choices I wanted to make about my life moving forward. I'm not sure if being forced to angrily spew all the resentment and confusion I had pent up inside of me about sacrifices made to fill a definition of what I was told a good person was, which were inbred in me as an impressionable child by Catholic instruction, or if the psychiatric magic of this amazing man had just taught me how to open that door I had walked into on the first day.

For the next few weeks we talked about clarifying my sense about my situation and how I would face and address my challenges. I think I knew shortly after the explosive session we had shared that my dependency on the good doctor was not what it had been. It came as no surprise when finally at a session he said, "I don't think you need to come any more. You can if you wish to. But you are a bright man and you know how to solve your own problems intelligently. We all make mistakes at times and you will. But you are able to stand on your feet again. You can always call me or set up an appointment if there is something you are genuinely struggling with. I don't think you will need it, but I offer it. You do not need my assistance any longer and prolonging continued sessions would be a misuse of both of our time. I wish you well."

I wanted to hug him. I think if I did he would have turned to sand or merely evaporated. He was not one to respond emotionally and I had too much respect to compromise his nature.

As I drove away I could see the cottage house in my rearview mirror. It slowly disappeared as I followed the road downward to join the traffic on Interstate 95. I didn't think this way back then but today I understand that I left guarded by the angel wings forged from this experience.

We all have our own realities. We all accept what is truth in our own personal way.

The secret to keeping our truths intact is to be open to new experiences and understandings, to not let one or two bad experiences define our understanding of anything. That practice keeps us sane and free to grow in whatever understanding of the world we outline for ourselves.

Fiction

Forever

> *Now, while we're here alone*
> *And all is said and done*
> *Now I can let you know*
> *Because of all you've shown*
> *I've grown enough to tell you*
> *You'll always be inside of me*

FOREVER
by Eva Ein Loggins, Kenny Loggins
& David Foster

The little boy sat on the soft cool sand of the beach as he pondered while looking out over the vast ocean before him. He would do this often. On many days he could be found here in the mid-morning sunshine or amidst the clearing mist and fog lingering from an early day storm. There was a quiet to all of this that, if nothing else, could make the boy smile deep within.

This morning he was feeling more serious about matters than he usually did in the hours that started his every day. The sun was shining brightly on the sparkling water. The sea foam rode in and out on the gentle waves as they caressed and massaged the shore. There was a kind of whispering that disrupted the otherwise deep quiet of the morning. There were no other people about. There were no seagulls screeching and scavenging for food. There were no boats on the horizon.

These were the perfect moments in time that the young boy most desired in his morning solitude on this vast and perfect beach. He came to this exact same spot daily to talk to the sea - to let the magic of this mighty power intermingle with his thoughts. And sometimes if there were things troubling his young mind, the ocean would relieve him of his confusions, taking them into the undercurrent and washing them away - out to sea.

There was an unspoken loyal understanding between the youth and the seemingly limitless expanse of his aquatic confidant. Only words held in thought and osmotic transference were shared between the mighty mentor and the ever-curious boy.

The elements of the young boy's world were particularly perfect and in sync with each other on this sunlit morning. The quiet and the privacy of this time, on this day, were profoundly unusual and especially vibrant. And the boy felt this.

As the young boy sat complacently in an unconscious harmony with all around him, he thought he heard a voice. He looked all around him, his world slightly rumpled but intact, but saw no one. Enough time passed for him to fall back into the effortless contemplative state he had been enjoying. Again, he heard a voice.

He took himself by surprise in recognizing that he felt no fear. This time he did not look around. He continued to sit quietly and listening. The voice came again.

"What is it that you are so eager to gain from your conversations with me today?" The Voice asked.

Steady but with a dust particle of trepidation, the young boy inquired, "Are you talking to me?"

"Yes." replied the Voice.

The boy recognized the Voice even though he had never really heard it before. "Why are you speaking out loud to me and not through our usual unspoken connection?" the boy asked. He knew it was the voice of the Ocean.

At first there was a thundering quiet. The boy was uncertain if the Ocean would answer. Maybe the directness of his question broke a sacred understanding of acceptance he had long shared with his strong and usually silent morning companion. But the quiet ended and the Ocean spoke.

"It is time in your understanding of the world that you recognize the difference between the kind of conversations and information we share that is only in your thoughts and true realities of ideas in the world in which you live and will grow older in."

The boy asked, "Is there a big difference?"

"That is something you will decipher for yourself when you learn and understand the strengths and frailties of just being alive." The Ocean compassionately told him.

"Hmm?" The boy vocalized as he scratched his head and wrinkled his brow as if those motions might help to explain this to him better, or at least allow him to comprehend this idea in the immediacy of this moment.

A month before this special sunlit day the young boy's grandmother passed away. He loved his grandmother very, very much and her now absence was troubling the boy more than perhaps he even knew. This was his first and only experience to date with the finite aura of death. Coming to terms with accepting that he would never see her again, never hear her voice again, never feel the warmth of her embraces that she showered on him with her hugs he loved so much, was a complex processing he was slowly learning to accept and understand. For acceptance and understanding are two very different things. The boy was doing well in grasping both better and better every day but the scars remained and the process was moving at a snail's pace. His quiet mornings with the crashing waves had been aiding his balance of his longing for his grandmother and his acceptance of this new difficult truth.

But in all the days of the past month, the boy never shared his thoughts on this with the ocean or the breezes that subtly whirled above the glistening water. Yet somehow, most of the weight of the sadness that was filling him was slowly eroding away. Likely, by a deeper subconscious osmosis, the sea was taking his sadness out into its depths on a strong and steady undercurrent.

As the boy surrendered more and more of his sadness by unknowingly dumping them into the sea, his concerns and questions about this matter were slowly being tended to, by his own resolving. The Ocean had absorbed the boy's sadness without the boy ever knowing he had shared it. Knowing what the boy had unburdened on his own, the Ocean was well versed on the current thoughts and issues churning in the boy's brain and heart.

And so the Ocean asked again, "What is it that you are eager to gain from your conversation with me on this particular day?"

This time the boy was quiet. Perhaps it was his innate shyness that formed the silence. Maybe it was an embarrassment he felt in perceiving the Ocean clearly knew more than what the boy had surrendered in their sharing. Most likely, he was formulating his answer as succinctly as he could from within his own muddled cognizance of what he truly sought.

It seemed like years before he finally spoke. Maybe it was. Then he said, " I have been very sad since my grandmother went away for good. I never thought much that something like this could happen. I am scared. I don't want other people or things that I love in my life to vanish and be gone forever. I do not like that this can happen. I want to cherish them *forever.*"

The last part of what he said was delivered with a swelling anger. Then the voice of the Ocean spoke quietly within the boy and directed him to re-find the calm he had before he spoke these words. And the boy began to feel safe once again.

There was a lengthy silence for several moments. Or maybe it was hours. It seemed like days. And the calm was found.

Not in audible conversation but through the telepathy they had always shared, the Ocean gifted the boy an understandable explanation that loss is inevitable in life and that we cannot prevent certain things from happening. And in the end the boy only *mostly* understood.

Then from a clear voice the sea wind went silent and the Ocean summoned what might have been interpreted as an offer of five wishes for things the boy could not bear to lose. The boy grew excited and no longer dwelt upon the wisdom the Ocean had just shared. He was confident his powerful mentor could provide the means for him to secure them in his life forever.

"As you name each one," said the Ocean, "you must tell me why each one is important to you. And when you are done I will take you to the future to show you the reality of what it is you think you desire."

The boy was overjoyed and rushed to begin speaking. The Voice interrupted him and reminded him, "Only these choices may stand as things within your ability to control as time and nature sculpt the future. You cannot redesign your choices. Once you have named five they will be your only choices where you can see what the future holds for them. Choose carefully."

"My parents!" Exclaimed the boy, "I want them to live forever with me." He made this choice with all the exuberance and confidence he held inside his very young soul. "Because I could not bear to lose them and relive the pain I have had from losing my Grandma."

"Are you sure?" questioned the Voice of the Ocean. And after a brief silence and the boy beaming with assuredness, "That's one," quietly stated the Voice.

EXTOLLING THE ORDINARY

The boy grew giddy as excited children do when they think they are winning at a game. Testing the Voice, he said, "Can I have a unicorn?"

"Why is that?" questioned the Ocean Voice, never acknowledging the frivolity or imposing an unspoken restriction upon the boy.

"Well, because they come from magic," hesitantly the boy worked to complete his reasoning, even though he was beginning to think he either wasted a choice or would be chastised for being silly. "They are bearers of hope and love and it would be nice to have such things in the world." the boy shyly finished, thinking perhaps he would be called out for not being as serious as this occasion was calling for.

"Done!" exclaimed the Voice, "that's two." And suddenly, there beside the boy on the beach stood a small gentle unicorn.

The boy stared at it in wonder and disbelief. He was a small bit confused for he did not imagine that such a thing could be real. While he was still a small child, he was enlightened enough to know that such things should not exist except in stories and other kinds of fictitious creations. He eventually accepted what had just happened and eagerly wanted to continue with his other wishes.

"My sister." he quietly said. "I choose her because even though we do not always get along, she is family and I know she will always be there for me."

"That is number three." The Voice riding on the ocean waves over the unnatural quiet replied.

"I know who is next!" The lad spewed out. "My best friend. Johnny! I can't imagine growing older without him to share all the fun and laughter and solving things together. Him for sure. That's a must"

"Four." The Ocean acknowledged. "And what will be your final choice?" it queried.

It took a while for the young boy to decide. He was being careful in his thinking. It may have even made his head hurt. More and more time passed in making this decision than in the previous silences as he had before the other choices. It is very possible that enough time passed in his making of the decision that the boy had actually aged enough to become considered a young man - perhaps no longer a boy. But he was still a child at heart.

It wasn't an expected choice but was seemingly a wise one. The young man stated, "My health. I will need that to be there forever for me to be able to share everything with all those I wish to have with me forever." And he looked out to sea where he could see a few small clouds floating on the landscape of the horizon.

In a quiet and consolingly kind voice, the Ocean said, "You have made your choices and now it is my obligation to take you where your wishes lead. This will take a lot of time. We no longer need to speak on the open wind to share what I will present to you." And as the morning sun moved further overhead and more clouds began to cast light shadows on the warming sand, the telepathic connection re-engaged between them, just as it had earlier in the morning and all the numerous mornings they had shared before.

As the young man sat upon the beach his mind was transported to a visionary place adrift somewhere between the sea and the sky. He could see himself in the future and how things were there. His first viewing showed him at fifty five years of age. The scene before him was not the warm oceanfront but that of a large cold stone mausoleum where he saw the plaque on the small sealed door with his grandmother's name engraved upon it. It was brass and shiny and glistened brightly along with the numerous others lined up and down the tall and wide wall of polished granite. As his eyes drifted downward scanning the names of others whose terminated lives were encased in this contemporary crypt, he saw the names of his parents, each with a brass plaque welded to the individual little doors.

"Why?" he exhaled through his rising grief and mounting tears. "This is not the promise of my wishes." And the tears that were falling from the young man's eyes were very real and flowing down his deeply saddened face. "This cannot be!" He decried. And he immediately though about his sister and the scene before him shifted.

He was standing in a supermarket and saw his younger sister, now in her early thirties, pushing a grocery cart. As he approached her, she pulled away from him, ignoring his advance as if she never knew him.

It seems about ten years earlier she had fallen in love with a young man that neither her parents nor her only brother approved of. She was guided by love and married the man. The marriage did not last long. Out of shame, regret, and deep disappointment she estranged herself from her family and chose to no longer engage with them. She preferred to only depend upon herself.

Learning this, no tears fell from the young man's eyes but he heard and felt a tremendous crack of thunder across his heart and it filled him with a great emptiness.

"How could this be? I did not wish for this," he ached inside to understand.

Pulling all the strength he could, he prepared himself and hoped for comfort in the vision of a future with his friend. "Where was Johnny?"

He hoped for the happier times as he felt himself returning to a younger time in his life. As he looked into the scene of the latest vision he could not see Johnny anywhere. The story unfolded that only a few years after the boy had his last exchange with the voices of the sea, Johnny's father received a huge promotion with his job which required that the family relocate all the way across the country. For almost a year the boys exchanged letters and on special occasions they called each other on the telephone. As they grew more and more into their teenage years their interests began to change and no longer sharing times together, they found their lives taking new shapes that were void of any influence from each other. And slowly contact ceased.

There was a brief period where the boy would sit on the beach and wonder if Johnny was sitting on a beach with a different ocean. "All the oceans connect." he deduced. But connection never happened. Even years later he tried to track Johnny down but was never able to follow through. Johnny's father's company moved them frequently and tracing grew more and more problematic. He stumbled on unverifiable stories that held grim reports of a premature demise of Johnny. But the boy would not take them to heart.

The young man grew deeply forlorn as he remained sitting on the beach looking over the rising tide before him.

The Voice sought to comfort him by explaining to him that no matter what one may wish for, there are givens in the world we inhabit that will always remain beyond human control. The very nature of life includes moments of loss, separation and disappointment. You cannot wish for things that defy the composition of what it is to be alive. Wishes are wonderful beautiful things. But not all wishes come true. Likely, most don't. The things we wish for are things we hold most dear to who we are. They remain important whether they come true or not.

The young man began to feel tired and very much older than he was. All this understanding of things he sought on his quiet beach were now weighing very heavy on him. He had become a little angry with his maritime companion. He knew he felt somehow betrayed but he wasn't sure why or by whom.

The voice of the sea had grown silent now that the sun was directly overhead. And the clouds that had been casting shadows had all cleared from the sky.

As he sat on the sand with the tides rising closer to him, he asked, "Are you still there my friend?"

A quiet answer came back, "*Forever.*"

The young man thought to himself, "I have certainly grown a great deal from what I learned today." And the truth is - he had. He learned to deal with truth no matter how harsh it could be. He felt different. Because he was. He was now a man in his late thirties. He was no longer a boy. He was no longer that young man he was when this story began.

As he recognized and adjusted to his current reality he noticed a hospital bracelet on his wrist that he had forgotten over days to remove. It showed that he had been a coronary patient in a nearby ICU.

"Not even my health." He exasperated, shaking his head.

And, in unison, the voices in his head - both his and that of the sea - said, "It's just good to be alive."

The man rose and faced the sea. He began to look around him and the beach had become filled with hundreds of people. There were children playing with pails and shovels. There were elderly couples gathering sea shells as they walked along the water's edge. There were families picnicking, young folks sunbathing, teams playing volleyball, bright colored beachballs floating through the air and occasionally bouncing off floral and striped beach umbrellas. There were folks in cabana chairs, others on blankets or towels. There were children and adults splashing around in the water. There were boats on the horizon. Overhead a sea plane flew dragging a kite banner behind it, advertising a local restaurant.

The man turned from the ocean to head home to join his wife and children. He made his way toward the dunes. About halfway there he turned back to face the water and he shouted loudly, "And where the hell is my damn unicorn?!?"

And the world around him stopped still. No one looked strangely at him. In fact, no one even heard him - everything went frozen in time. It was like his world was as it was before. There was nothing moving or apparently alive except for him and his Ocean.

Then, in a firm and loud voice, not in the man's head, but rumbling over the rushing tide came this:

"YOU STILL HAVE IT. IT IS WITH YOU."

"I don't see it." said the man.

"Of course you don't." said the Ocean. "You knew when you asked for it that they were not real. But you still wanted it because of all the hope and magical possibilities the lore of that creature holds. Everything that magical creature stands for lives within you. You created and made these things - the caring for your parents, your love for your sister even though she will not requite it, the happy memory of your first best friend - you will always have these and more with you - *forever*. You created the unicorn and only you can make it go away."

EXTOLLING THE ORDINARY

And the Voice went quiet.

"Are you still there?" asked the man.

But there was no answer in his ears or in his head. And while the world around him regained it's pace and the sounds and motion of everyday life returned, he turned again and walked toward the dunes, where he could see the looming structure of a rather characterless resort hotel that had swallowed the land where his childhood home once stood.

Afterword

> *What's it about?*
> *Did I lose innocence going in*
> *Or gain experience coming out?*
> *What did it mean?*
> *What have I learned?*
> *Eatin' off tables before they're turned*
> *Livin life instead of playing dead*
> *Throwin' down the pencil and grabbin' a pen*
> *Takin' the wheel - drivin' again*
> *Throwin' down the pencil and writing in ink*
> *This is how I feel - this is how I think*
> *Dreamin' again and makin' those dreams real*
>
> "Taking The Wheel"
> music & lyrics by John Bucchino

I don't have a lot to say now that my second volume of stories, essays and poems has reached completion. I pray the writing stands for itself. I hope the entries show a growth from me as a writer but still hold to the simple ideas that people said they liked in my first book. There are no diary entries in this volume. Well, maybe *Broad Stripes and Bright Stars* could qualify. I also have no story guised as a letter like the final entry in *Etchings*. I faced my storytelling head on in this book. If I couldn't tell something outright, it went in a "maybe later in another book" file. There are still stories from and about my life that I have yet to figure out how to tell. I will get to them. For now, there is one story that very much needs to be told - and so I will get to it right here, right now.

This is the story of my cherished friend and incomparable editor, Matthew DeCapua.

OK, he screwed up the opening format of this book by writing a Foreword without being able to come up with a song that may have inspired it. Or so he claims. *My* telling of his story, regarding this, is that when he saw that the poem I wrote on the birth day of his first child, a beautiful daughter, was being included in this volume without a song lead-in, he felt competitive, and that he was entitled to the same exemption because, well, because he is Matthew DeCapua, "The Captain." While I had to do some serious mental adjusting about MY book being upstaged in the opening pages by HIS brilliant writing, and by using his own format, I found comfort in my knowing even though there are lighthouses mentioned throughout his piece, it wasn't inspired by a Jimmy Buffet song or the Village People's "In The Navy." I credit him with being smarter than I thought by his concealing his questionable taste in music.

All kidding aside: If I had to write a story about Matt, I would not know where to begin. All I can do is admit that this book would definitely not be here without him. Being a new father, working his regular office job, preparing his auditions for his acting career, and staying on top of hundreds of details in getting his film produced, his days are too short to get it all done. Yet more amazing than the Energizer Bunny he goes on - 24/7. And still he found time to read my drafts and show me my endless mistakes of spelling, sentence structure, and punctuation, and when something just didn't make sense as I thought it did. He could have, and maybe should have, walked away from doing this for me. But he didn't.

I could never replace him. He is the most astute grammarian I know. And despite even knowing that, I argue against and ignore his input far too often. I have been blessed to have his skills to guide me, and more blessed that he respects my desired uniqueness in how I express myself in literary terms. Often the conflict is gargantuan but he always helps me find the way to express myself that feels like my authentic voice. When we don't agree he will let me have my way. More than he knows, his corrections to my manuscripts spark rewrites that better express what I initially set out to say. He is the best guide I could possibly have in allowing me to wander off the path yet somehow get home quicker. And he does it all with a sense of humor that keeps my self-frustration in check.

The opening statement of his return of the final draft said, "…good news - your usual problem with hyphenated words this time around is far less…bad news - your ability to use a comma is waaaayyyyy worse." We still battle over verb tenses. I'm stubborn. I don't concede easily or often. I want my writing to be like how I talk and I guess I drift in and out of time as I think and write. So those mistakes, as with the last book, are solely mine. This time around his skill in roping in my abstract comparisons has been invaluable. Readers are spared hundreds of moments that might have caused them to scratch their heads until they bleed. There are still hundreds there - but don't blame him.

In my writing, I regularly allude to the religious value I attribute to friendship. I confess, Matt is the earth angel whose friendship has kept me on track for over twenty years. He is the Seraphim of all the angels who guide me and look after me. Blessed by his friendship, I am indebted to him for whatever positive attention my books may get.

Matthew - next time please come up with a song or I will tell little Lucille when she grows up that you were petty enough to compete with her before she could defend herself.

I also need to thank Atticus for his companionship and not eating me. How did I ever live without a cat - especially this one? And thanks to my loving daughter for dropping this sharp-clawed and itchy-toothed little furball into my life like a tornado in a trailer park. Happy to report, there have been no lives taken and all damages are reparable.

Again, I thank the composers and lyricists whose brilliance I have noted for my inspirations. None of you sued me last time around but my fingers are still crossed and I still say my prayers nightly. I am indebted to you and offer a profound thanks to you all.

Mostly I want to thank everyone who read *Etchings on Angel Wings* and decided to continue on this journey with me in *Extolling the Ordinary*. And I thank those of you who have made the effort to embrace me for the first time. I am honored by your interest. I haven't figured out yet if the angels want a vacation from me or if they will hang with me for more of my etchings. Time will tell. I will be back - I do feel an inclination to explore more fiction next time around.

No feather dropping from above this time telling me to write more, but my child within is wanting another outing. Somehow I feel it's not ice cream he is asking for this time. One of the issues with children growing up is that their wants become more expensive. So please buy my books and recommend them to others so I don't have to disappoint him!

It's never *The End*

About the Author

Kevin Thompson was born in Waterbury, Connecticut. He now resides in New York City. The son of the late Michael Bernard Thompson and Arlene Humiston Thompson, he was educated in public schools and graduated Cum Laude with a Bachelor of Fine Arts degree from Denison University and a Master of Fine Arts Degree with honors from Ohio University. He started writing while in high school where he was the editor of the school newspaper. In college he continued his journalistic writing, first as the fine arts writer and reviewer for the college newspaper, and then became the fine arts editor. His writing there merited him an induction into The Society for Collegiate Journalists, then known as Pi Delta Epsilon.

Kevin has worked in the entertainment business for almost five decades. His work as a stage director has been seen across the United States. He has served as a stage manager for several nationally recognized theater companies. He has taught in some of the leading institutions of theatrical training as well as serving as a private coach in New York City. His service as a talent agent and personal manager has spanned a thirty year period. He has worked for major casting companies. He recently served as a designer for an independent short film that is getting recognition on the indy film festival circuits.

His first anthology of stories, poems and essays, *Etchings on Angel Wings,* was published last year and is available in both book and ebook forms on Amazon. He is currently at work on a novel and a play.

He has a brother who resides in southern California and a daughter who resides in Connecticut. His cat, Atticus, tends to rule his life.

Made in the USA
Middletown, DE
30 September 2021